A Dynasty of Love

Tila gave a cry and shrank away from the handsome American.

"No . . . no!" she cried. "How can you . . . ask me to do anything so . . . wicked?"

Clint Wickham took a handkerchief from the pocket of his robe and wiped Tila's tears away very gently.

"I am sorry—so very sorry," he said. "You cannot be so cruel as not to forgive me!"

He took her hand in both of his, and because he was touching her he felt Tila quiver.

"I want more than I have ever wanted anything to kiss you, but I will behave as you wish me to. Goodnight, my darling."

He bent his head and kissed her hand.

It gave her a strange feeling in her breast that she had never felt before . . .

A Camfield Novel of Love
by Barbara Cartland

"Barbara Cartland's novels are all distinguished by their intelligence, good sense, and good nature . . ."
—ROMANTIC TIMES

"Who could give better advice on how to keep your romance going strong than the world's most famous romance novelist, Barbara Cartland?"
—THE STAR

Camfield Place,
Hatfield
Hertfordshire,
England

Dearest Reader,

Camfield Novels of Love mark a very exciting era of my books with Jove. They have already published nearly two hundred of my titles since they became my first publisher in America, and now all my original paperback romances in the future will be published exclusively by them.

As you already know, Camfield Place in Hertfordshire is my home, which originally existed in 1275, but was rebuilt in 1867 by the grandfather of Beatrix Potter.

It was here in this lovely house, with the best view in the county, that she wrote *The Tale of Peter Rabbit*. Mr. McGregor's garden is exactly as she described it. The door in the wall that the fat little rabbit could not squeeze underneath and the goldfish pool where the white cat sat twitching its tail are still there.

I had Camfield Place blessed when I came here in 1950 and was so happy with my husband until he died, and now with my children and grandchildren, that I know the atmosphere is filled with love and we have all been very lucky.

It is easy here to write of love and I know you will enjoy the Camfield Novels of Love. Their plots are definitely exciting and the covers very romantic. They come to you, like all my books, with love.

Bless you,

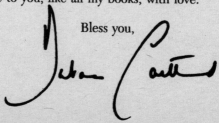

CAMFIELD NOVELS OF LOVE

by *Barbara Cartland*

A NEW CAMFIELD NOVEL OF LOVE BY

BARBARA CARTLAND

A Dynasty of Love

J

JOVE BOOKS, NEW YORK

A DYNASTY OF LOVE

A Jove Book / published by arrangement with
the author

PRINTING HISTORY
Jove edition / January 1992

ISBN: 0-515-10757-3

Jove Books are published by The Berkley Publishing Group,
200 Madison Avenue, New York, New York 10016.
The name "JOVE" and the "J" logo
are trademarks belonging to Jove Publications, Inc.

10 9 8 7 6 5 4 3 2 1

Author's Note

IN 1874 there began the rush of English and European Aristocrats to America to entice with their titles American Heiresses into becoming their wives.

There had been throughout American history occasional marriages of Heiresses to Noblemen.

In the nineteenth century Elizabeth Astor, the daughter of John Jacob, had married Count Vincent Rumpff.

That started a bargaining sale with Jenny Jerome marrying Lord Randolph Churchill.

In the following years Heiresses came from all parts of the country with Fifth Avenue in New York being the leading supplier.

In 1904 a Goelet girl married the Duke of Roxburgh. The Earl of Yarmouth, who became the Marquis of Hertford, obtained an Heiress and received a million dollars for doing so.

Perhaps the most famous marriage of all was that of the Duke of Marlborough to Consuelo Vanderbilt, who was reluctantly forced up the aisle by her ambitious mother.

chapter one

1882

T ILA looked round the Drawing-Room and saw that the wallpaper was peeling in one corner.

There was a new damp patch on the ceiling above it which had not been there before.

She sighed.

There was no chance of it being repaired.

She supposed that, like other ceilings in the house, it would get worse and worse until it collapsed.

It depressed her to think of it.

She walked to the window to look out onto the wild, unkept garden.

The only consolation was that the oak trees in the Park were as beautiful as they had ever been.

A profusion of daffodils were coming out in a golden carpet beneath them.

The Spring always brought her hope, but each year things seemed to get worse.

She had wondered despairingly when she went to bed last night how they could survive.

It was not only herself, but Roby and the two

elderly servants, who were all they had left.

The Coblins had been at Staverly Park for over forty years.

They had started as Boot-boy and Dairy-Maid in the kitchen.

They had risen over the years until Mrs. Coblin was Cook to Tila's father and mother, and Coblin became the Butler.

He had three footmen under him.

Mrs. Coblin had three maids in the kitchen and two in the scullery.

"The Good Old Days!"

How often Tila had heard people say that, and, where she was concerned, it was what they had been.

She could remember as a child how lovely the house had looked when her mother entertained.

The carriages drawn by well-bred horses had come driving up to the front-door.

The guests would emerge glittering with jewels and dressed in the latest fashion.

To Tila, peeping through the bannisters, they had looked like people in a Fairy Tale.

Her mother, wearing the Staverly Tiara, had undoubtedly been a Queen.

She could hardly bear to think of it now.

Although the tiara was still there, so much else had been sold.

All that remained were the pictures of their Staverly ancestors, which were entailed.

That applied to everything else that was left—the silver, the inlaid cabinets, the magnificent collection of armour, and, of course, the early editions in the Library.

"And what is the use of them for the son I shall never be able to afford to have!" Roby had said furiously the last time he had come home.

He was living in London to be with his friends, out to enjoy himself as much as he could, though he had no money.

Hostesses were delighted to ask a handsome, un-attached young Baronet to their parties.

They certainly did not want a girl who could not afford a roof over her head or a single gown in which she could be presented at Buckingham Palace.

Tila therefore stayed in the Country.

She had not minded as long as she had her horse to ride.

Now, without enough money even to pay for food, she was becoming desperate.

She knew it was no use pleading with Roby.

She was quite certain, although he was too ashamed to admit it, that he was already in debt, if only to his Tailor.

Neither Roby nor she could appeal to their relations.

They had either died or else were themselves in particularly straitened circumstances.

"Have the Staverlys never had money?" she asked Roby the last time he was at home.

"The first Baronet was able to build this house," he replied. "The next two or three improved it, and our grandfather, curse him, spent a fortune on it!"

"What was the point of making it so big," Tila asked, "if there was no money to run it?"

"I suppose there seemed a lot at the time," her brother replied, "and Papa had money when he first inherited."

There was a contemptuous note in his voice.

It was always there when he spoke of his father.

Tila could understand why he was so bitter.

Sir Osmund Staverly, the 5th Baronet, had been a very handsome, dashing man.

He had been content to live in his magnificent house and on his large estate as long as his wife was alive.

But when she died, he had gone back to the life he had enjoyed when he was young.

Tila had really not quite understood what he did.

She thought there had been a number of attractive "actresses" with whom he enjoyed himself.

For some reason she could not ascertain, they were very expensive.

There had, of course, been horses, carriages, Phaetons, and Curricles.

Some of the horses had come down to Staverly Court.

But a great number in which Sir Osmund was interested were only to be seen on a race-course.

Apparently he could never resist a bet.

"He spent all the money," Roby went on, "on slow horses and fast women!"

Tila did not quite understand.

But she did know the enormous amount of debts her father left.

He had been shot in a duel which had something to do with a woman whom her brother described as "fast."

Duelling was forbidden by Queen Victoria, but of course it still took place in secret.

Tila could not bear to think of her handsome, attractive father setting out for Green Park at dawn, only to meet his death.

The man who had killed him had gone abroad.

He would doubtless be able to return in three years.

But there was no return for Sir Osmund.

It was a shock to her, and she knew it was a shock for Roby, who was just leaving Oxford.

He had never anticipated the manner in which he found himself as Sir Robert Staverly, 6th Baronet.

"I am left," he said furiously, "without a penny with which to bless myself!"

His father's creditors had accepted grudgingly 10 shillings in the pound.

That was attainable only by selling everything that could be realised.

These were not only the contents of the house, which left blank places on the walls.

They also had to sell part of the estate which, fortunately or unfortunately, had been added only in the last fifty years.

This contained three of the best Farms, also cultivated land which had brought in a certain amount of income from the crops.

They were left with woods which, while Tila loved them because they were so beautiful, were unsaleable.

There was pastureland, but there were now no horses to graze on it.

There was the village which housed the pensioners from the Big House.

They, when they retired, were given cottages after years of faithful service.

It was not only Staverly Court that was now in a deplorable state.

The cottages in the village leaked and lacked panes of glass in every window.

The gates into the small gardens needed rehanging and were broken or missing.

"I am ashamed to go into the village!" Tila had said to Roby six months earlier.

"If I do not have a new suit of evening clothes," he replied, "I shall not be able to accept the invitations I receive for dinner and I shall go hungry!"

"What are we to do?" Tila had asked miserably.

"God knows," he replied, "because I have no idea."

He had gone back to London, taking a carpet which he thought he might sell for a few pounds.

As far as they could see, it was not on the list of items that were entailed.

"I suppose somebody would find out if I took the tiara and sold that!" Roby said. "If I pawned it, I might get a good price!"

Tila gave a little cry.

"You dare not do that!" she said. "That horrible Solicitor, who for some unknown reason was made one of our Trustees, comes every three months to see if anything is missing."

She stamped her foot before she went on:

"I hate him! I usually go out for the day when he comes. He pokes his nose into everything!"

"I suppose he is only doing his job," Roby said. "When I think what that First Folio of Shakespeare is worth, I feel like selling it and risking the row!"

"There would not be a row, there would be a scandal!" Tila replied. "And you know as well as I do that if it got into the newspapers, the smart hostesses with whom you spend so much time would remove your name from their lists."

"Those 'smart hostesses,' as you call them," Roby retorted, "certainly provide me with luncheon and dinner. I have reached the stage now where I cannot afford breakfast!"

Tila thought she could not afford any meal.

If it had not been for the rabbits, the pigeons, and the ducks on the Estate, she and the Coblins would undoubtedly starve.

Her father had taught her to shoot when she was a young girl.

Although she hated doing it, she had to do so in the woods, otherwise there would be nothing to eat.

Coblin, although his rheumatism was bad, planted potatoes and a few vegetables.

They grew among the weeds in what had once been a large and luxurious kitchen-garden.

But he was finding it difficult to work outside.

It was becoming more and more necessary for Tila to have to shoot everything, otherwise they would all have gone to bed hungry.

"We cannot go on like this," she told herself.

But what was the alternative?

She could not think of one.

Although she prayed and prayed, it seemed as if God had forsaken her.

She looked round the Drawing-Room, thinking how lovely it had looked when her Mother had entertained there.

The tapers in the crystal chandeliers had been lit.

There had been flowers from the hot-houses which her Mother arranged because she loved to do so.

Then, Tila thought, there had been horses in the stables.

Now there was only Kingfisher, who was getting old.

She loved him because she had ridden him ever since she was a child.

At the same time, she wondered despairingly what she would do when he could no longer carry her.

With Kingfisher she could escape from the dust and decay in the house and ride into the woods.

There she would tell herself fairy stories of finding treasure hidden under the trees.

Perhaps she would discover some rare species of tree which horticulturists had been seeking for many years.

The stories she invented and those she read in books in the Library were in fact her only companions.

After her Mother had died and her Father went to London, there was no more entertaining at Staverly Court.

The neighbours were no longer interested in the Staverlys.

In the last year since she had grown up, she had not been invited to a single party, nor had anyone called at the house.

"Why should they want me?" she had asked. "And if I did receive an invitation, what would I wear?"

There was no answer to this.

She talked about it to Kingfisher because there was nobody else to listen.

"I might as well be on a desert island," she told him.

He nuzzled against her as if he understood and was trying to comfort her.

She flung her arms round his neck and said:

"If you were only a magical horse, you would make something happen. As it is, you are just a dear old 'Fuddy-Duddy,' but I love you!"

She had been riding that morning, and it was impossible for her to ride him again.

She had gone into the garden, where the flower beds were just a tumble of weeds.

But the lilac bushes were coming into blossom and the almond trees were already pink and white.

Kingfisher followed her as if he were a dog, and Tila was comforted by the beauty of it.

She had told Kingfisher that they had nothing to eat.

After she had taken him back to the stable, she had come to the house.

Now she turned towards the door.

As she did so, she heard somebody in the hall and wondered who it could be.

She was quite certain that at this time of the afternoon Coblin had his feet up.

He would be snoring in the arm-chair which he had taken into the kitchen.

Curious, she walked out of the Drawing-Room.

Then she gave a cry of sheer delight.

It was Roby who was standing there.

Behind him through the open door she could see, to her astonishment, a smart Curricle drawn by two horses.

She ran towards her brother, her arms outstretched.

"Roby! Roby! You are here! How wonderful!"

She flung her arms around his neck and he kissed her, saying as he did so:

"I thought you would be pleased to see me. How are you?"

"Depressed, until I saw you!" Tila answered. "Why have you come home? What has happened?"

"A great deal," he answered, "and I have a lot to tell you. But first let me tell Coblin to show my groom the way to the stables."

Tila's eyes widened.

She knew, however, that for the moment there was no point in asking her brother questions.

She left Roby and ran down the long passage which led to the kitchen.

She pushed open the baize doors outside the Dining-Room.

Then she ran over the flagged floor to open the kitchen door.

As she expected, both Mrs. Coblin and her husband were asleep in the arm-chairs.

They had originally been in the Writing-Room.

Just for a moment Tila hesitated.

She knew how much they enjoyed their afternoon nap.

But Roby was home, and that was far more important than anything else.

She touched Coblin by the shoulder.

"Wake up," she said gently, "Sir Robert is here!"

"Eh? What d'you say?" Coblin asked hazily.

"Sir Robert—he has arrived back and he wants you to show the groom the way to the stables."

"Sir Robert—back?" Coblin muttered.

As he struggled to his feet, his wife opened her eyes.

"If Sir Robert's back, Miss Otila," she said, "there's nothing for dinner, as ye well knows!"

The Coblins always called her by her proper name.

They thought "Tila" disrepectful.

"We will find something," Tila said confidently, "but let me speak to Sir Robert first. I do not even know if he is staying yet."

Coblin got to his feet.

He was putting on his coat which he had put over the back of one of the kitchen chairs.

It was threadbare and darned in several places.

At the same time, once it was on, he looked as he always had—a family Butler who knew the etiquette of a big house from the scullery to the attics.

He smoothed his few remaining white hairs into place.

Then he walked with his usual dignity from the kitchen and along the passage to the hall.

Roby was waiting there.

He was looking at a painting of the house which

hung beside the grandfather clock.

It had been done a hundred years ago, when the Georgian alterations had been made.

Tila often looked at it, but it was depressing to realise that Staverly did not look the same now.

Roby was staring at it intently.

He only turned round as his sister and Coblin joined him.

"Good-afternoon, Sir Robert!" Coblin said.

Tila always thought his voice made him sound pontifical, like a Bishop.

"Nice to see you, Coblin," Roby replied. "Will you show my groom where to stable the horses? He will have to sleep in the house. As you know, the stable roof leaks."

"Very good, Sir Robert," Coblin said, without showing any surprise.

He walked to the front-door and down to where the Curricle was waiting.

"If you are intending that you and your groom are to stay," Tila said, "I only hope you have brought something with you to eat. There is nothing—and I mean nothing—in the house!"

"I guessed as much," her brother replied, "and I have brought a hamper filled with good things, starting with *pâté de foie gras!*"

Tila stared at him.

"Who gave you that?" she enquired.

"I bought it!"

There was silence, then Tila asked:

"Are you . . . joking?"

"No, and I have quite a lot to tell you," her brother

answered, "but let us go somewhere where we can sit down. Incidentally, I have also brought some champagne for us to drink!"

"I think I am dreaming!" Tila said, "unless you have suddenly—overnight—become a Millionaire!"

"Very nearly," Roby replied.

"Now I know I am dreaming!" Tila answered.

She led the way into her Mother's Sitting-Room, which was exactly as it had looked when she was alive.

This was because the French furniture it contained could not be sold.

Nor could the pictures which had been bought by their Grandfather after the French Revolution.

He had duly entailed them onto the next Baronet.

The sun was coming through the windows and, although the curtains were faded, the room looked very pretty.

Yesterday Tila had arranged a vase of narcissus and a larger one of white lilac.

Roby moved to stand with his back to the empty fireplace.

Tila shut the door, then she said:

"You look very smart!"

"I thought you would admire my new coat," her Brother said. "It was the first thing I bought."

Tila sat down on one of the Louis XIV armchairs.

"Start at the very beginning." she said. "You must know that I am . . . dying with . . . curiosity!"

"I think you will find it hard to believe what I

have to tell you," Roby said, "but our fortunes have changed overnight!"

"But . . . how? How can they have done?" Tila asked.

"I have let the house!" Roby replied.

"*Let* it? To whom? And how could . . . a stranger . . . live in it as . . . it is now?"

The words seemed to tumble out of Tila's mouth, and her Brother laughed before he said:

"I was just as astonished as you are when Patrick O'Kelly told me what he had done."

Tila had heard her Brother speak of his friend Patrick O'Kelly before.

She knew he was the younger son of the Earl of O'Kelly, an impoverished Irish nobleman.

She remembered Roby had told her how Patrick made himself useful to all sorts of distinguished people.

It was through Patrick he had been a guest at house-parties to which he would never have been invited otherwise.

He had also been asked to innumerable entertainments which he had enjoyed.

"How could Patrick O'Kelly have let the house?" Tila enquired. "And if he has, who would pay rent for it in the state it is now?"

"That is exactly what I asked him," her brother replied, "and the answer is simple—an American Multi-Millionaire!"

Tila gasped.

"Is that true . . . really . . . true?"

"Cross my heart, it is the truth!" Roby replied.

"But it is the most exciting thing I have ever heard!" Tila exclaimed. "Now—start from the beginning."

It was obvious that Roby was only too willing to do so.

"As I have told you before, Patrick, because he has no money, makes himself indispensable to a great number of interesting people. It is a kind of joke in London when people say: 'If you want something from a Unicorn to a rich Banker, Patrick will get it for you!' "

Tila laughed, then she said:

"Go on!"

"I do not think I told you," Roby continued, "but Patrick went to America just after Christmas. It was with a very rich, attractive member of the Vanderbilt family—but that is a different story."

He had obviously suddenly remembered to whom he was speaking, and went on quickly:

"Naturally, Patrick made a lot of contacts in New York. As I expect you know, a large number of the British and European nobility have been looking for brides amongst the Millionairesses with which, apparently, that City abounds."

Tila knew nothing of the sort.

Her Brother saw the expression in her eyes and explained:

"I could give you a whole list of the English Aristocrats, and of European Barons and Counts who are pecking amongst the dollars like a lot of greedy cockerels!"

Tila was listening with a rapt expression on her

face, but she did not interrupt.

"Well, trust Patrick to find something new!" Roby continued.

"What is . . . that?" Tila asked because he obviously expected it.

"The reverse side of the coin," Roby replied. "Now an American Millionaire wants a distinguished English wife, the daughter of a Duke, if possible!"

Tila laughed.

"It sounds ridiculous!"

"Not as far as we are concerned," her brother said.

"You mean . . . renting this . . . house?"

"Exactly! So that he can look at the Marriage Market, and you may be quite certain that Patrick will find him exactly what he needs."

"But how can he . . . take the house . . . as it is?"

"That is just the point. We have one month in which to make it look as it did when our Grandfather lived here."

"And . . . he will . . . pay?"

"Of course he will pay!" Roby asserted. "He is so rich that King Midas would be a beggar compared to him."

"How is . . . that . . . possible?"

"Anything is possible in America," her brother replied, "and Patrick tells me that Clint Wickham— that is his name—inherited an enormous fortune from his father, and owns half the Railways in America."

He drew in his breath before he continued:

"And now, because money always goes to money, his land in Texas, which is where he comes from, has been found to contain more oil than has ever been discovered before!"

"It sounds . . . for us . . . too good . . . to be . . . true!" Tila cried. "There must be a snag."

"Stop being a 'Doubting Thomas'!" her brother ordered. "Patrick has got it all fixed. We will make the house perfect, and as it was always meant to be. We will have to install a number of bathrooms, but that is what we might have expected."

"Bathrooms?" Tila echoed.

She had never seen a bathroom.

In her Father's day, stalwart young footmen had carried huge brass cans of hot and cold water up the stairs.

The baths had been put in the bed-rooms and the occupants bathed in front of the fire.

Now, when she wanted a bath, Tila had to tell Coblin.

He would bring one of the cans to the office which had once been used by a Secretary.

It was conveniently near the kitchen and on the opposite side of the passage to the Dining-Room.

But because of his age and his rheumatism, it was somewhat of a commotion.

Usually Tila washed in cold water which she carried up the stairs herself.

"Patrick thought," Roby was saying, "that we should put in ten bathrooms. That should be enough to start with."

"But there are not enough rooms!" Tila objected.

"Do not be silly!" her brother retorted. "There are the Powder Closets and several of the best bed-rooms

17

have Wardrobe-Rooms. Of course we may have to convert one or two Dressing-Rooms."

"How can he possibly need so many bathrooms?" Tila enquired.

Her brother smiled.

"Americans are very clean, and if Clint Wickham does not have bathrooms, he will not have Staverly."

"Then let us give him bathrooms and anything else he wants!"

"That is exactly what we are going to do," Roby said, "but we will have to hurry. What I want to know is the name of every builder, carpenter, painter, and repairman in the whole Country."

"I should think Coblin would know that better than I would," Tila replied.

"Yes, of course," her Brother agreed, "and I can go and ask that old boy in the village, if he is still alive, who used to do repairs here in Papa's time."

"You mean William Emerson," Tila said. "He is alive, but very slow."

"We shall need all the help we can get," Roby said, "and the first thing they can do is to repair the window in my room. There was a ghastly draught last time I stayed here!"

"You are welcome to any other room," Tila answered, "but there is something wrong with every one of them!"

"Everything has to be 'made good' and quickly!" Roby retorted.

"I have not asked you how much he is paying," Tila said, "and I suppose that is the most important question of all."

"Hold your breath," her brother replied, "because it is quite fantastic!"

"Tell me," Tila begged.

"He will pay for all the repairs, the curtains, the cutlery, the carpets—everything that is required, and, for as long as he stays here, he will pay us two thousand pounds a year!"

Tila gave a cry which seemed to echo round the room.

Then she jumped to her feet to throw her arms round her brother's neck.

"We are . . . saved! We are . . . saved!" she cried. "My prayers have been answered . . . and it is all . . . due to . . . you! How can you have been so clever as to have Patrick O'Kelly as a friend?"

"He has been useful to me before this," Roby admitted, "but I never thought anything could be so fantastic!"

"That is exactly the right word," Tila enthused, "and now that Mr. Wickham is our tenant, we can move into the Dower House."

She smiled before she went on:

"I have always loved that little house, and it is not in anything like as bad repair as the state we are in here. Of course, we must take the nicest of Mama's possessions with us, including the furniture from this room."

Because she was so excited, her voice had a lilt in it which sounded like music.

She suddenly became aware that her Brother was looking at her with a strange expression in his eyes.

He did not speak, and after a moment she asked:

"What . . . is . . . it?"

"I suppose in this world nothing is quite perfect," he replied, "and there is a condition to everything I have just told you."

"A . . . condition? What . . . sort of . . . condition?"

"I am afraid you will not like this," Roby said uneasily.

Tila sat down again in the chair.

"What is it?" she asked. "Surely Mr. Wickham cannot be asking for anything . . . frightening?"

"It is not Mr. Wickham."

"Then . . . who?"

Tila knew her Brother was feeling for words before he said:

"Patrick fixed up this deal not only for himself originally, but with a man in New York who has found him useful in the past."

"I . . . I do not . . . understand," Tila said.

"I will try to make it clear to you," Roby said in an irritated voice, "but it is not easy."

"Why . . . not?" What is . . . wrong?"

"The truth is," her Brother said, "this friend of Patrick's is very eager to be associated with Wickham's enterprises, or Investments, if you like, which invariably are so successful."

"Why does he not ask Mr. Wickham to let him become a partner in his Company?" Tila asked.

"Apparently Wickham works on his own and has no wish to have partners or to share the knowledge of his Investments with anybody else."

Tila looked puzzled and Roby went on:

"What this friend of Patrick's has asked for is that

somebody at Staverly while Wickham is here keeps their ears open. If they have the slightest idea of what Wickham is doing next, or in other words, where he is putting his money, Patrick should be informed."

"It sounds to me very . . . complicated," Tila said. "I cannot think how . . . you can be . . . expected to find somebody whom Wickham does not know, and I should have thought anything of the sort would be far . . . beyond the . . . head of any . . . servant."

"Yes, of course," her Brother replied, "and that is why at Patrick's suggestion I have agreed that the only person who would not make a mess of it would be . . . you."

"Me?" Tila exclaimed. "What am . . . I supposed . . . to do?"

"That is what I am going to tell you," Roby replied, "but you keep asking questions!"

Tila thought this was rather unfair.

She clasped her hands together and raised her face towards her Brother.

"Clint Wickham," he said slowly, "has a daughter."

"You did not . . . tell me he was . . . married!" Tila exclaimed before she could prevent herself.

"He is a widower. His wife died four years ago and his daughter is aged seven."

There was a pause, and, as Tila did not speak, Roby went on:

"One of the reasons he wants a really nice house with an Estate is because his daughter is coming to England with him, and Patrick had been told to find her a Governess."

There was silence.

Tila's eyes widened, and with difficulty she repressed herself from speaking.

"Because the person in the house," Roby continued, "must be someone Patrick can trust, you, Tila, will be the Governess to Wickham's daughter!"

Tila stared at him. Then she said:

"What you are . . . really saying is that you want me to be . . . a spy. The answer is 'No,' definitely 'No'! How can I . . . possibly do . . . anything like . . . that?"

Roby made a gesture with his hand.

He then walked across the room to stand at the window, looking out at the garden.

"I am sorry, Roby," Tila said, "but you know it is . . . something Mama would never . . . approve of me doing. And anyway . . . I would . . . make a mess . . . of it."

There was a long silence. Then Roby said:

"Very well, the whole deal is off, and I only hope you can afford to go on living here with no money!"

"It is . . . not that," Tila expostulated, "but . . ."

"Incidentally," Roby went on without turning round, "Patrick gave me a thousand pounds for advance expenses. I have taken five hundred of it myself, and have five hundred here for you!"

"Five hundred . . . pounds!" Tila whispered beneath her breath.

She could hardly believe it possible that she could possess so much money.

She knew that the first thing she would do would be to pay the Coblins' wages.

They had not received any for nearly a year.

Then she would buy some decent oats for King-fisher.

Half the reason why he was so weak was not because he was old, but lacked proper food.

It was not only food that the Coblins wanted.

They were, she knew, terrified that the house would have to be closed.

There would be nowhere for them to go except to the Workhouse.

They knew better than anyone else that there was no money with which to pension them off.

Even if there was a dilapidated cottage available, they could not live in it without money.

"Five hundred pounds!"

She told herself the sum was written in flames of fire on the wall in front of her.

"Five hundred pounds!"

If Roby had not taken the precaution of bringing some food with him, there would have been nothing for dinner to-night.

She looked at the back of her brother's head.

He was seeing, as she was, what a difference five hundred pounds and the money that was to come after it would make to them:

Two thousand pounds in rent, the house back as it had been when it was first built.

The gardens with their lawns sweeping down to the lake in perfect repair.

The kitchen-garden, that big, walled-in acre of

weeds, planted with vegetables.

The greenhouse would be repaired.

There would be grapes, peaches, greengages, and cherries.

It would be just as it had been when she was a child.

If she said no, if she refused to be put into what she thought was a humiliating, untenable position, who would be impressed?

Roby was still silently staring out the window.

Tila felt his disappointment, and resentment came towards her like a wave of the sea.

She felt as if it swept over her and was drowning her.

Finally, she could bear the silence no longer.

In a small, quavering voice he could only just hear, she said:

"What . . . else do you . . . want me to do?"

He turned round.

"Do you mean that? Do you really mean that?"

"I shall . . . make a mess of it . . . then you will be . . . angry with me!"

"If you make a mess of it," he said as he walked towards her, "at least we will have had the house repaired and still have some of the rent. I will have it put in the contract that we are paid monthly."

He reached the chair in which she was sitting and looked down at her.

"I am sorry, Tila," he said, "but, honestly, there is nothing else I can do but agree to Patrick's suggestion."

"It . . . frightens me!" Tila murmured.

"I know," he replied, "but it will not be as bad as you might think. For one thing, you do not have to be yourself."

Tila started.

"Not myself? What do you mean?"

"It was Patrick's idea that you should help us, and he thought it would be a terrible mistake for Wickham to know that you are my sister."

"Why should it be so . . . terrible?"

"For one thing, because I have promised Patrick to help him introduce Wickham to the Social World in which he expects to find his aristocratic bride."

"Oh . . . I see . . ." Tila said. "Therefore he would not be very . . . impressed to find that your sister is just . . . a Governess!"

"No, of course not!" Roby agreed. "And that is why you will have another name, and just be one of his employees."

He paused before he added:

"But you will be in the house. You will be able to know who comes and goes, and if there is any talk of Investments, or new Companies—things like that."

Tila parted her lips to say that she had no intention of reading papers or letters that were not intended for her.

Then she said nothing.

She thought the whole idea was horrifying.

At the same time, it was not a question of what she wanted or did not want.

It was a question, quite simply, of survival.

As if Roby could read her thoughts, he said:

"If you refuse, and of course I understand what you are feeling, Patrick was talking of finding a house South of London, in any case. There are a number, I am told, that would suit Wickham equally as well as this."

Tila gave a little sigh.

She knew quite well that her Brother was making it clear that she actually had no choice but to comply.

She had to accept their conditions, horrifying though they might seem.

As she had thought before, it was a question of survival.

Not only for herself, but for the Coblins and—Kingfisher.

chapter two

IT was three days after Roby had started going round the County looking for workmen that Tila made her own conditions.

The first thing she had done when Roby handed her the five hundred pounds he had promised her was to pay the Coblins the wages they were owed.

They almost wept with delight.

She knew then that whatever happened, she could not abandon them.

She also told William Emerson in the village to keep one man back from working on the house to repair the cottages in the village.

She put aside one hundred pounds for this.

The rest she knew she must bank for the emergencies which would certainly arise in the future.

She was not certain how much Roby would allow her from the rent.

He had said optimistically at dinner:

"You will be paid for being a Governess, and that will at least provide you with new clothes."

"New clothes?" Tila said in surprise.

Then she laughed:

"I suppose no one would be impressed with a Governess who was patched, darned, and looked like an old scarecrow!"

"That is true," Roby agreed, "and you should certainly smarten yourself up a bit, not that Wickham will notice you one way or the other."

"Not if he is inspecting Dukes' daughters!" Tila smiled.

It was as Coblin was serving them with some of the delicious dishes that Roby had brought with him that she said:

"I have a condition to make. As I accepted yours, Roby, it is only fair that you should agree to mine."

"What is it?" her Brother asked.

She knew he was nervous in case she backed out at the last moment.

"As Mr. Wickham will want younger servants," she said, "we have to have somewhere for the Coblins to go. I have already ascertained there are no empty cottages in the village."

"So what are you suggesting?" Roby asked warily.

"That we install them in the Dower House. Then, if you wish to come and stay for a short while, it is there for you, and also for me, if I get dismissed!"

"That would be a disaster!" Roby exclaimed.

"It may be. At the same time, I will have to have somewhere to live," Tila said logically, "and where better than the Dower House, which we both love?"

"It is certainly an idea," Roby agreed.

"It is my condition for doing what Patrick O'Kelly wants," Tila said firmly, "and it would be a mistake to leave the Coblins here calling me 'Miss Otila,' whatever new name Patrick has chosen for me."

"Very well," Roby agreed, "that is settled. Have it your own way."

"Thank you," Tila answered, "and the rest of my condition is that I move some of Mama's special treasures into the Dower House, especially her things from the Blue Sitting-Room."

Roby did not answer, but she knew he was not going to make any difficulties.

The next day she went over to the Dower House to see what was needed.

It was very attractive, having been built in the reign of Queen Anne.

It was of red brick with elaborate carvings over each of the windows.

The rooms were not very large but had high ceilings and the polished floors were in good condition.

The ceilings were certainly in better shape than those at Staverly.

The furniture was mostly what had been there since the time the house was built.

The curtains were in bad condition.

But the windows were much smaller than those in the Big House.

Tila thought they could use the best parts of the curtains from there as they were replaced with new ones.

They would certainly not be good enough for the fastidious Mr. Wickham.

The more she heard about him, the more she thought that however much of a benefactor he might be to them, he was an unpleasant man.

"Why is he coming to England to find a wife of social importance?" she asked Roby.

"According to Patrick," Roby replied, "Clint Wickham's mother was an Englishwoman."

That was a surprise, but Tila did not say anything.

"Apparently," her Brother went on, "he adored his Mother, and she told him tales of England and about English people which he has never forgotten."

Tila thought that sounded reasonable, and Roby continued:

"When he became immensely rich he decided to build a Dynasty of his own so that the Wickhams would always be respected on both sides of the Atlantic."

"I suppose if he is getting old," Tila said, "what he wants is a son, or several of them."

"Getting old?" Roby repeated. "Why do you say that? Wickham is a comparatively young man!"

Tila was surprised.

"I thought as he is so involved in big business, he would be forty at least!"

Roby laughed.

"He is just over thirty. They start young in America, and he apparently took over his father's business as soon as he was grown up."

"Then if he is young," Tila questioned, "I cannot understand why he cannot fall in love with a pretty American girl and not want to be a social celebrity."

"He can manage both with all the money he has," Roby answered, "and of course Patrick has said he will introduce him to the Prince of Wales."

Tila was not surprised to hear that.

Roby had told her that there was considerable controversy in London because the Prince asked all sorts of different people to Marlborough House.

He included those who had never been accepted in Royal Circles before.

As if Roby were following her thoughts, he said:

"His Royal Highness likes them rich, and as Wickham is very, very wealthy, he will be welcomed with open arms!"

Tila thought the whole idea was rather unpleasant.

She realised the vast amount of money that was to be spent on making Mr. Wickham comfortable at Staverly Court.

She found her dislike of him growing day by day.

Tila knew she ought to be grateful.

Yet it annoyed her to see how eager Roby was that everything should be right.

Patrick O'Kelly arrived unexpectedly.

He drew up in a smart travelling carriage.

It was drawn by horses which she knew that he could not have afforded to buy.

It meant he had either borrowed them or else Mr. Wickham was paying for them.

He was a pleasant-looking Irishman with the traditional charm that was characteristic of those who came from the "Emerald Isle."

He paid Tila compliments which came automatically to his lips.

She knew, however, that he was looking with a critical eye at everything that was being done to the house.

Roby was certainly achieving miracles.

The workmen had no regular hours.

They started with the dawn and ended when it became too dark to be able to see what they were doing.

"They have repaired the roof," Robert said proudly to Patrick, "and have now started on putting back the fallen ceilings. I have also hired an excellent Artist to come and restore those that are painted."

Patrick O'Kelly inspected everything and was even complimentary about the meals.

Tila had already engaged two women from the village to help Mrs. Coblin.

It was not that she was worried so much about what she and Roby had to eat.

At least they could now afford the best meat.

But the kitchen was invaded at all hours by the workmen.

They wanted something hot to drink and often begged "a bite o' food."

Tila could afford to pay for extra help.

But she was being very careful in case their "Nest Egg" should disappear overnight.

Roby had bought some good wine for Patrick to drink.

However, when he arrived he contributed half-a-dozen bottles of champagne.

After dinner they sat in the Blue Sitting-Room on which the workmen had not yet started.

"You have done wonders, Roby!" Patrick said. "But I must warn you, I have heard from my friend that Wickham might arrive earlier than we expected!"

"He cannot do that!" Roby exclaimed.

"He will if he wants to, and nothing will stop him," Patrick replied, "so be prepared!"

Roby groaned.

"There is still much to be done, and we have not yet chosen all the furnishings!"

"I am sure your Sister is helping you," Patrick said.

He smiled at Tila as he spoke.

She thought once again he was going to pay her one of his fulsome compliments.

She had been aware ever since he had arrived that he had been scrutinising her.

It was as if to make sure she was the right person to carry out his instructions.

She felt herself stiffen before he went on:

"I am sure your Brother has told you, Miss Staverly, how very important you are to the success of this venture?"

Tila did not answer, but waited, and Patrick continued:

"If Wickham is not satisfied with the house or with anything else, he is quite likely to wash his hands of the whole thing and go somewhere else."

"For God's sake, we must not let him do that!" Roby exclaimed. "With the money he is paying for the rent, he can, as far as I am concerned, stay here indefinitely!"

Tila suppressed a cry of horror.

33

She could not bear to think of anyone, especially an American, living forever in what was her home.

Of course it was wonderful that it was being restored.

At the same time, she was saying a little prayer.

It was that, when it was all done, Roby would be able to marry a girl who had enough money for them to live there.

He had said so often that he could not have a son and heir.

Yet she had always hoped that by some miracle he would be able to live at Staverly and have a family.

Then it would be just as it had been in her Father and Mother's day.

She had not really thought of herself, except to suggest jokingly that if she lived alone with only Kingfisher for company she would become an "Old Maid."

Now, with so much talk about Mr. Wickham's marriage, she kept thinking of Roby.

It struck her strange that she had never heard of him being in love with anybody while he was in London.

But then, he never talked much about his private affairs.

Surely, she argued, there must be a woman of some sort in his life?

Perhaps, like her Father, they had been "fast," and she was therefore not supposed to know about them.

After what Patrick had said, she looked across the room at her Brother, who was saying:

"We have to keep Wickham happy, Patrick, and I

know you have plans as to how you will do so."

"We will have big parties here, once the house is ready and he has moved in," Patrick said, "and I think from all I have heard about him, he would rather entertain than be entertained."

"Then we will need horses."

"I was going to talk to you about that," Patrick replied. "There is a sale on at Tattersall's next week, and I want you to come up to London to start filling your stables."

Roby's eyes lit up.

"I will enjoy that!" he said. "But I hardly like to leave the workmen to their own devices."

"I am sure your Sister knows exactly what to do and what to say," Patrick suggested.

"I suppose so," Roby admitted somewhat reluctantly.

"I will do my best," Tila answered, "but if anything goes wrong, do not blame me!"

Patrick got up from the chair in which he was sitting.

He crossed to the sofa to sit down beside Tila.

"I want to talk to you," he said, "about your part in all this."

Roby also rose.

"While you are doing that, I will just slip upstairs and see how they are getting on in the Master Suite."

Roby had gone from the room before Tila could say anything.

As he shut the door she felt somehow shy.

At the same time, she was resentful at what Patrick was going to say to her.

"I know you will be able to do everything your Brother wants of you," he said in his beguiling voice which had a touch of Irish brogue in it.

"I have agreed," Tila replied, "but, quite frankly, I am very nervous in case I fail."

"I am sure you will not do that," Patrick replied. "I cannot say too often that everything depends on you."

"I do not know . . . what you mean," Tila answered.

Patrick moved away from her.

She knew he was thinking of how much he should tell her and that it might be a mistake to say too much.

She waited, thinking she was like a small fly being caught in a big web of intrigue.

"You do understand," Patrick said, "that my American friend who has arranged for me to look after Clint Wickham when he comes to England is extremely influential, and also a very demanding man?"

Tila did not look at Patrick, but he knew she was listening.

"He wants full value for his money," the Irishman went on, "and if he does not get it, he can, I am assured, be very unpleasant."

"Are you . . . suggesting he may . . . threaten . . . me?" Tila asked.

"No, no, of course not," Patrick answered quickly. "But Americans can be over-temperamental when it comes to making money."

"What do you mean by . . . temperamental?" Tila enquired.

Patrick made a gesture with his hands and said quickly:

"There is no reason to go into details. All I am begging you, Tila, and it is impossible for me to go on calling you 'Miss Staverly,' is to find something—anything—that will make my American friend happy."

"And if I do not?" Tila asked. "And my name is Otila."

She saw no reason why a stranger should use the name she was called only by her parents and Roby.

There was silence before Patrick replied:

"Then, of course, Otila, we will have all failed!"

Tila had the idea that he had been going to say something completely different.

He added quickly:

"But I know perfectly well that it is something you will not do, and as you are so lovely, I feel you will make a success of anything you undertake."

"I hardly think my looks are of any importance," Tila replied. "I am only hoping my brains do not betray me!"

Patrick laughed.

"I have only just thought of it," she added, "but I suppose Mama would be very shocked at my staying in the house where the host is a bachelor and I have no Chaperone."

"That would be true if you were a guest in the house," Patrick answered, "but you have to remember you are now an employee, and Mr. Wickham's only concern will be whether or not you can look after his daughter and are an adequate teacher."

He saw that Tila was still looking worried and went on:

"I do not want to be rude, but however beautiful you are, you do not qualify for the 'Wickham Stakes.' The only runners allowed to enter are the daughters of Dukes and Marquesses, perhaps a Princess thrown in as the 'Favourite'!"

Tila laughed, as he expected her to do.

"Of course I am not even an 'Also Ran,' " she said, "which certainly makes everything easier."

"Not only easier but socially correct," Patrick said. "And you can believe me when I say I am an expert in this sort of intrigue."

Tila wanted to reply that she had no wish to be involved in any intrigue.

But the die was cast—she had accepted the situation, and that was that!

Later she went round the house with Patrick and Roby.

She had to admit that it was exciting to be able to spend as much money as they wanted.

Staverly Court was beginning to look more magnificent than it had ever been before.

When they came downstairs, the man Roby had employed to do the curtains was waiting to see him.

Looking at the silks, satins, and velvets he intended using made Tila admit that the house was more important than her own feelings.

When she went to bed, she told herself that she and Roby should be very grateful to Patrick O'Kelly.

She thought, however, that being Irish, he would

take risks without counting the cost, also without asking if he was doing anything dangerous.

She had the uncomfortable feeling that that was what Roby was undertaking, without his being aware of it.

She had read that Wall Street, when there was a Monetary Crisis taking place, was like a battlefield.

If that was true, she was entering into a situation where money counted more than anything else.

She herself might be in the "firing line."

Then she laughed at her own imagination.

Whatever happened, whatever she did or did not report back to Patrick, who was to know?

It was very unlikely that anyone would suspect that a young, unimportant Governess was involved.

At the same time, she was afraid!

She sent up a prayer to her Mother and Father, asking them to take care of her.

* * *

"Personally, I am exhausted!" Roby said, throwing himself down on a sofa.

"Oh, do be careful!" Tila cried. "That has only just been finished. If you make it dirty, there will be no chance of having it cleaned."

Roby had been working in the house all day.

He had not only told the workmen what to do, but had lent a hand wherever it was wanted.

Three weeks had passed since they had started putting the house in order.

It seemed to Tila sometimes as if it were more like three years.

Patrick had come down several times to spur them on.

He wrote to Roby almost every day, suggesting something else.

It would be something he wanted done, or made new. His suggestions were almost impossible.

He had written yesterday:

I thought the garden could be improved with a fountain. I have seen a magnificent one which came originally from France. It would only cost £1,500 and I think you might like to put it somewhere where it can be seen from the windows of the Drawing-Room.

As Roby finished reading the letter he groaned.

"How the devil does Patrick think I am going to have time to fix up a fountain?" he asked. "We would have to run the water from somewhere, and, if it comes from the lake, we can hardly expect it to run uphill."

"I should forget Patrick's suggestio⋅ ̈ Tila replied.

She was not certain, however, if her Brother would follow her advice.

Patrick had sent them horses before half the stable buildings had been repaired.

He had also sent down a carriage and a very smart Chaise when there were no out-buildings ready to house them.

"I am going to write to Patrick to-day," Roby said, "and tell him that the main rooms of the house are finished, and if Mr. Wickham arrives, he will have to put up with the men still working on the Second Floor and on one of the wings."

"I cannot think why Patrick cannot ask him to stay with one of the Dukes to give us more time," Tila murmured.

"If you ask me," Roby replied, "Patrick will keep him in London for as long as he can. After all, he has rented a house for him there, and he has a lot of people lined up for him to meet."

"That is the first cheerful thing you have said!" Tila exclaimed. "And I suppose now that the house is nearly finished, we should start thinking about how to staff it."

"Patrick is seeing to all that," Roby replied.

"You did not tell me!" Tila said reproachfully.

"I forgot!" Roby answered. "But he has already arranged with a Butler who was with the late Duke of Newcastle to engage the footmen. I understand he has found a French Chef who is supposed to be one of the best in the Country to take over the kitchen and do all that is necessary."

"What about a Housekeeper?" Tila enquired.

"I am sure Patrick has got one up his sleeve," Roby answered. "Do not worry yourself, but make sure the School-Room and your own bed-room are comfortable."

Tila laughed.

"I have done that. My bed-room really looks lovely! You must come up and see it, Roby. I shall enjoy being in the rooms where we were so happy when we were children."

Her voice softened as she said:

"One of my earliest memories is of you riding the Rocking-Horse, and wishing I could ride it too."

"You will have to make certain that Wickham allows you to ride his horses, at least when he is not there," Roby said. "The one I rode this morning was sheer joy!"

Whatever else he was doing, Roby was always up early enough to have an hour's ride before breakfast.

The Country air, and because he went to bed early had made him, Tila thought, look better than she had ever seen him, and certainly more handsome.

When he had first come down from London he looked tired and somehow dissipated.

She knew that late nights and heavy drinking were bad for him.

Now he looked a different man.

She thought she might say the same for Kingfisher.

She had been right in thinking that the reason he seemed old and tired was that he was being badly fed.

Now, with the horses they had bought for Clint Wickham, he was having the best food obtainable.

So Kingfisher had taken a new lease on life.

Nevertheless, Tila enjoyed riding the new horses.

Yet she always felt a little guilty in case Kingfisher resented it.

She had been riding in the woods.

Everything in the past three weeks had come into blossom.

It was all so lovely that she thought that anything was worthwhile.

If she had to crawl under the beds, dive into the lake, or listen behind doors, she would not complain.

Roby stretched and said:

"Moving the furniture into place has made me feel sticky. I am going to have a bath."

"Is the hot water really working?" Tila enquired.

"It was yesterday," Roby replied. "What was your water like this morning?"

"Still rather tepid," Tila replied. "But it is very exciting to see it pouring out of the taps, so I am not complaining!"

Roby laughed.

"If you have a bath before dinner, we can compare notes," he said, "and I shall be extremely angry if the water is not piping hot!"

He went from the Sitting-Room as he spoke and did not hear his Sister reply.

She was saying how strange it was that they should be complaining about hot bath water.

For years she had been obliged to wash in cold.

She looked around the room.

It had a new carpet, new curtains, and the French furniture had all been repaired.

The cushions on the sofas and chairs had been re-covered.

An expensive blue silk brocade had been set into the original Louis XIV frames.

"Mama would have been delighted!" she told herself.

When she reached the bed-room in which she was sleeping she remembered that she had a new gown hanging in the wardrobe.

It had just been delivered from the Dressmaker in the village.

After what Roby had said, Tila had bought some cheap material from the Carrier who came by once a week.

She had asked him if when he next called he would bring something more expensive in the colours she desired.

He was a very obliging man who served all the villagers round about.

He brought Tila some very pretty blue silk as well as a roll of white gauze which he told her was a "snip."

"There be a slight mark on every yard," he explained. "It won't show when 'tis made up, an' it be marked down t' 'alf-price!"

Tila had thanked him and taken it to the village Dressmaker.

She gave her a picture which she had cut out of the Ladies' Magazine to show her exactly what she wanted.

Mrs. Saunders had done a good job.

Tila could have made it herself, but Roby needed her with him almost every minute of the day.

He did not entirely trust his own judgement on the colours for the walls.

He asked her about the materials for the curtains.

Together they decided the way the furniture should be arranged in the rooms.

So many things had been sold from the house that in some cases they had to start furnishing "from scratch."

They had driven to the nearest big Town.

Then they had found most of the things they required at what Tila considered reasonable prices.

"Mr. Wickham ought to be grateful this is not costing him as much as he might have expected!" she said.

Roby gave her a sidelong glance.

Because she knew him so well, she exclaimed:

"Is Patrick charging him more than we are actually spending?"

"Of course!" Roby said. "He has to make something out of all this."

Tila gave a sigh.

"I had no idea that he would be taking a commission on the furniture!"

"He considers it his right to take a commission on *everything*," Roby declared, "and 'everything' is the right word. After all, he set up the deal and makes all the arrangements."

"That is true!" Tila agreed. "At the same time, it seems a complicated way of living."

"Nobody knows that better than I do," Roby said, "but if it is a question of being poor or rich, I much prefer being rich!"

"Of course!" Tila smiled. "But there are certain things a Gentleman should not do."

"That depends upon whether you are a Gentleman with empty pockets and expensive tastes," Roby said curtly.

There was silence before Tila said:

"Have . . . you done the . . . same sort of thing . . . yourself?"

Then he replied a little gruffly:

"Of course I have! If somebody asks me to buy them a horse, I expect them to pay for my knowledge and experience of horse-flesh. It is far easier to put a little more on the price of the horse than to ask for it separately."

"I . . . suppose I . . . understand," Tila said doubtfully.

She was thinking that Roby would never have done anything like that if he had not met Patrick O'Kelly.

She had a terrifying feeling that without meaning to they were both sinking into a kind of quicksand.

One thing led to another.

It was very different from when her Mother had been alive.

Then the world had seemed a wonderful, simple place with the sun shining every day.

"I am asking too much," Tila told herself.

At the same time, she was afraid of the future.

chapter three

TILA went to the School-Room and looked out over the Park.

Like everybody else in the house, she was feeling apprehensive because Mr. Wickham was arriving to-day.

It had been merciful that he had spent a fortnight in that house in London before coming down to Staverly Court.

Roby had gone to join him. Tila's last words to him were:

"Keep him away from here for as long as you can."

"I doubt if anything I could say would have the slightest effect on 'His High and Mightiness'!" Roby replied.

Tila thought that was the right way to describe him.

She had found herself growing more and more resentful every day they worked on restoring the house.

It was wonderful, of course, to see it altering under their hands.

It was becoming the beautiful Palace she had thought it to be when she was a child.

At the same time, it irritated her that Roby was so concerned with making it perfect not for himself, but for a stranger.

She was quite certain when he did come Mr. Wickham would be brash and very unappreciative.

Why should he like anything that was so English and a part of history?

"He will just take it for granted," she told herself, "and doubtless compare it unfavourably with his ranch in Texas."

Yet when she saw the velvets and satins against the windows, and the new carpets Patrick sent from London, she wanted to sing with joy.

Staverly was beautiful! Staverly was impressive!

Staverly was as exquisite as their Grandfather had wanted it to be.

He might have spent a fortune, but it was nothing compared to the money Mr. Wickham was spending now.

At first Roby had been a little hesitant about buying things he felt were too expensive.

Then, when Tila told him he was being stupid, he almost, she thought, went to the other extreme.

At the same time, everything they had purchased looked exactly right in the rooms that were painted and gilded by a Master's hands.

Now at last the moment that she dreaded was upon them.

Roby had written three days earlier.

His letter said that he and Patrick were bringing Mr. Wickham and his daughter to Staverly on Wednesday.

Tila had stared at the letter as if she felt it could not be true.

She supposed in her heart she had always hoped at the last moment Mr. Wickham would change his mind and go back to America.

It was very unlikely, and yet such things did happen.

Her imagination told her that perhaps an Oil Rig would blow up, or two of his trains would run into each other.

Then he would have to return to where he had come from.

Before the new servants arrived at Staverly, she had moved into the Dower House with the Coblins, and, of course, Kingfisher.

She had made it look very attractive with some of the furniture from the Big House.

She had also, as she had thought originally, persuaded the man who was arranging the new curtains to give her the old ones.

Because she had asked him so nicely, he had even hung them for her, and made new pelmets.

The Dower House therefore was looking, she thought, very attractive.

She disliked having to leave it to go and do her duty at Staverly.

It had been difficult explaining to the Coblins that they were never to mention her existence to any of the new staff.

She had finished by saying:

"It means I shall earn enough money to enable us to live comfortably. You will get your wages and good food because Sir Robert has arranged for me to look after the new tenant's little girl."

"Does this mean, Miss Otila, you'll not be livin' here wi' us?" Mrs. Coblin asked in astonishment.

"Not while Mr. Wickham is in England," Tila replied, "but as he owns vast possessions in America, I do not suppose he will stay here for long."

This seemed to appease the Coblins, but they murmured something about it not being the same without her.

She had left the Dower House that morning.

She had repeated to them several times that now that they had said good-bye to her, they were not to mention her name again.

"Them in t'village'll think it strange, you workin' up at t'Big House, Miss Otila!" Coblin said.

"They will not know I am there," Tila answered, "for the simple reason that I am changing my name."

Both the Coblins stared at her in astonishment.

"Changing your name, Miss Otila? Why should you do that?"

"Sir Robert thought it would be embarrassing if our tenant knew that I was his Sister."

The old couple thought this over for a moment. Then Mrs. Coblin said:

"There's some sense in that, after you've made it look so pretty an' all."

Tila thought that was hardly the right adjective to

describe the magnificence of Staverly.

But all that mattered was that the Coblins agreed to keep silent.

Roby had already ordered a carriage from the Livery Stables in St. Albans to pick her up from the Dower House.

She was ready with her luggage when it arrived.

She looked, she thought, very English and exactly as a Governess should.

As she drove the short distance to Staverly, she paid the driver.

There was then no chance of him talking to the Butler or footmen who would meet them at the door.

"I was told t'expect you, Miss Stevens," the Butler said in a courtly fashion. "I hope you 'ad a good journey?"

"Very good, thank you," Tila replied.

The footman escorted her upstairs to the Floor which she had furnished so attractively.

As she went she was thinking of how much she disliked the name Stevens, which Patrick had chosen for her.

"Why 'Stevens'?" she asked petulantly. "I think it is a horrible name!"

"I chose it with care," Patrick replied, "because the first two letters are the same as yours. I was not certain if your initials might be engraved on your luggage or any other possessions."

"No, they are not," Tila replied, "and I would like a more attractive name."

"It is too late now," Patrick replied. "I have already written asking my friend in America to tell Clint Wickham I have engaged exactly the right Governess for his daughter."

Tila thought resentfully that he might have consulted her before he did so.

She realised before she spoke that Roby was frowning.

He wanted her to accept everything that was being done without complaint.

All the same, she thought, if the Almighty Mr. Wickham's daughter was as spoilt as he was, she obviously had a very difficult task ahead of her.

Now, as she looked out of the window, she could see the drive stretching away under the oak trees.

Shortly, the carriages in which the party from London were travelling would arrive.

She still somehow thought of Mr. Wickham as being the old man she had expected him to be before Roby had enlightened her.

She did not believe the stories that he was so brilliant.

How could he manage such an enormous fortune unless he was old, not only in mind, but perhaps in outlook?

"No young man," she told herself scornfully, "would want to marry a woman just for her title and her Family Tree."

As for creating a Dynasty of his own, she had never heard of anything so ridiculous.

Then she decided she would unpack her clothes.

She must be ready to devote herself entirely to her pupil when the child arrived.

The School-Room was large.

It had been chosen as a Nursery for Roby and herself by her Mother so that they could romp about.

Two rooms opened out of it, one of which had been her bed-room, the other Nanny's.

Across the landing there was one other bed-room which had been Roby's.

It looked out over the garden.

His room caught all the afternoon sun, while in the Nursery the sunshine poured in at breakfast time.

Tila had been tempted to sleep in the room that had been her own.

Then she felt she would be happier being able to look at the garden, especially now that it had changed so miraculously.

Roby had engaged eight gardeners.

They had been working as energetically as any of the other men he employed to make the gardens perfect.

The lawns were smooth and like velvet; the flower-beds were a riot of colour.

After all Roby's protests, the fountain had been installed and was throwing its water up to the sky.

What had delighted Tila more than anything was that the great yew hedges had been cut.

They had once been a perfect example of Topiary and gave the garden a feeling of magic which she had loved when she was a child.

At the far end she could just see from her bed-room a cascade running down from the woods. It ended in a large pool.

The rock garden around it had been planted with

exotic flowers which were now in bloom.

She had taken only a quick glance from her bedroom when she had come upstairs.

Now she went from the School-Room and across the landing.

It was an unexpected surprise to find there was a maid already there, unpacking and lifting her dresses into the wardrobe.

"Oh! You are doing it for me!" Tila exclaimed. "How very kind!"

"The 'Ousekeeper asks me to maid you, Miss," the girl answered, "an' also to look after th' young lady when she arrives."

"What is your name?" Tila asked.

"Emily, Miss, an' I'm ever so pleased t'be 'ere!"

She spoke so enthusiastically that Tila smiled.

"I hope we will all be very happy together."

"It'll be strange workin' for an American gentleman," Emily said. "Do you think 'e'll 'ave feathers on 'is head an' do strange dances like they told us when I were at School?"

Tila laughed.

"You are thinking of the Indians who were the first people to live in America, not the Americans themselves. Mr. Wickham will undoubtedly look more or less like any English gentleman."

Emily looked disappointed.

"I was lookin' forward to seein' someone wiv feathers!"

It struck Tila as very funny.

At the same time, she told herself, Mr. Wickham

54

might be more unpleasant than a Indian Chieftain would have been.

It was not something she could say aloud.

Emily took the last of her belongings out of her trunk.

When Tila found she had more time than she expected, she ordered several more dresses to wear during the day.

The Dressmaker also made her two plain but attractive gowns for the evening.

There was no likelihood of anybody seeing them, for she would dine alone in the School-Room.

She felt, however, that her Mother would have been shocked if she did not change for dinner.

It was what she had always done when her parents had been alive.

Now, of course, she could have a bath in the impressive bathroom which Roby had added to the Nursery Floor.

It had originally been the small bed-room which housed a Nursery-Maid.

It was difficult to recognise it now with a large bath in it, and the walls decorated with a pretty paper.

Surprisingly, the floor was carpeted.

"Why a carpet?" she asked her Brother. "Surely it will get wet?"

"Patrick told me that when he was in America and staying with the Vanderbilts and other important families, there were carpets on the bathroom floors. He was therefore certain that was what Mr. Wickham would expect."

There were carpets, Tila found, not only in the Nursery bathroom, but everywhere else in the house.

She only wished her Father could have seen the house as it looked now, before he died.

He would have been delighted.

She prayed that when Mr. Wickham returned to America, she and Roby could move back into Staverly.

Yet they would need a lot of money not to let it lapse into the tumbledown condition it had been in two months ago.

"Please . . . God . . . please," she prayed as she walked round the great rooms.

It seemed greedy to ask for more.

But how could they ever remain as they were if there was not enough money even to keep them dusted?

Then she told herself she was asking for too much.

She had not known where the next meal was coming from.

Then, as if Patrick had waved a magic wand, he had arranged for one of the richest men in America to be their tenant.

"I am . . . grateful, I am . . . grateful!" she told herself over and over again.

She tried not to think of the future, but just to be content with the present.

Her unpacking was finished.

Emily left her, saying she would bring her tea at four o'clock.

"If there be anythin' you wants, Miss, jus' tell me an' I'll ask Mrs. Danver for it."

"Is Mrs. Danver the Housekeeper?" Tila asked.

She knew the answer, but she thought it would be a mistake not to appear ignorant.

"Yes, Miss, an' 'er's ever so nice."

Tila smiled.

She realised that everything was new and exciting to Emily.

She was not prepared to be critical of anything.

Tila was glad to have someone young and enthusiastic to look after her.

She looked out at the garden for quite a long time, then moved back into the School-Room.

Just as she reached the window she had her first glimpse of a carriage coming up the drive.

It was followed by several other vehicles.

There were also two outriders.

Clint Wickham was arriving in style.

The leading carriage crossed the bridge over the lake.

It came up the short incline which led to the courtyard in front of the house.

Tila knew that the new red carpet would have been run down the stone steps.

Four of the six footmen would be waiting.

The Butler would be in the doorway with two others behind him.

It would be a well-rehearsed pageant.

She only hoped that Clint Wickham, as an American, would appreciate it.

* * *

As the carriage passed over the bridge Roby looked out of the window.

He saw first the smoothness of the green lawns, then the crimson carpet on the steps.

He turned to Clint Wickham, who was sitting beside him.

"I have arranged for the servants to be waiting to greet you in the hall," he said, "and you understand I will introduce them to you."

"Yes, of course," Clint Wickham replied, "and Patrick tells me he has chosen servants who have been in the very best houses."

He spoke almost perfect English and only one or two words had a slight American accent.

Patrick, sitting opposite, smiled.

"I have taken a great deal of care," he said, "in making sure you will be properly looked after, and nothing is better than the attention you can get from a good servant in England."

"That is what I have always heard," Clint Wickham answered.

The carriage which was drawn by four horses came to a standstill.

A footman wearing the resplendent livery of the Staverlys and a powdered wig opened the door.

Mr. Wickham got out first and the footman bowed.

As Roby and Patrick followed Clint Wickham, they walked up the steps to where Burton the Butler was waiting.

"Good-afternoon, Sir!" he said to Clint Wickham when he reached him. "May I on behalf of the staff welcome you to Staverly Court?"

"Thank you!" Clint Wickham said.

Then Patrick, because he had engaged the servants, introduced Burton, the six footmen, and Mrs. Danver with what seemed an army of housemaids behind her.

Then there was the Chef, also with a formidable retinue, and finally Mr. Trent.

Mr. Trent was the Secretary who would oversee the household and the Estate on Mr. Wickham's behalf.

He was the only member of the staff Patrick had allowed Roby to choose.

"You must make him understand he is to look after the Farms and see that the gardeners are adequate," he said. "Make it clear any expenditure should not go directly to Mr. Wickham but pass through my hands first."

Roby understood this meant only one thing.

The Secretary must not ask too many questions about how things were arranged while Mr. Wickham was present.

Clint Wickham had shaken hands with the Senior Servants and nodded to those behind them.

Then Roby took him through the main rooms on the Ground Floor.

The Drawing-Room looked beautiful with flowers arranged on every available table.

The sun was shining through the windows.

The fountain which had given him a headache was performing outside in the garden.

Clint Wickham made no comment.

They passed from the Drawing-Room into the Study which had been completely re-furnished.

The old red leather arm-chairs had been hopelessly beyond repair.

A number of sporting pictures which had been the delight of Sir Osmund had not been entailed.

On Patrick's advice, Roby had replaced them with pictures he bought at Sotheby's.

One over the mantelpiece, which was a very attractive Stubbs, seemed exactly right for the Study.

Roby hoped fervently that when Clint Wickham's tenancy was over he would not take it away with him.

"This is the room my father always used," he said as Clint Wickham looked round. "You will find it comfortable and I should make it clear that when you are in here you do not want to receive visitors."

"Do you think I will have many?" Mr. Wickham enquired.

"Everybody in the neighbourhood will call on you if only out of curiosity," Patrick said before Roby could speak, "and, of course, when you have a party you may want a place to escape."

Clint Wickham did not reply.

They moved on to the Card-Room, the Billiard Room, and the Writing Room. The magnificent Library was next, with its new red velvet curtains and particularly fine Persian carpets.

Now it held a great number of newly-bound volumes which replaced those which were too faded and tattered.

"I hear, Staverly," Clint Wickham said, "you

have some early Folios of Shakespeare and other ancient authors."

"That is true," Roby replied, "there is a Catalogue of them, although I am afraid some of the newest volumes here have not yet been included."

"I should be interested to see the Catalogue," Clint Wickham said.

Roby gave it to him and he carried it when they left the Library and went into the Blue Room.

Although Clint Wickham looked round, he said very little.

When they returned to the large Drawing-Room, tea was ready for them.

It was then he looked at the clock.

"I should have thought Mary-Lee would have been here by now!" he remarked.

"You told me half-past-four," Patrick said quickly, as if Clint Wickham was finding fault.

"Yes, of course," he answered, "but I hope they have no difficulty in finding the way."

"I am sure you can trust the coachman," Patrick replied, "and your daughter would have been disappointed if she had missed the luncheon which was given specially for her."

"Yes, of course," Clint Wickham agreed, "it was very kind of the Duchess. At the same time, I would have preferred her to come with me."

There was a faintly mocking smile on Roby's lips at what was being said.

He knew that Patrick had gone to immense trouble to arrange that the Duchess of Warminster should give a special luncheon for Mary-Lee.

Her youngest daughter was the same age.

Needless to say, she had another who was eighteen.

Lady Letica had been introduced to Clint Wickham almost as soon as he had arrived in London.

Patrick had been certain she would capture him.

Then it would be a waste of time to arrange for him to meet any other girls.

She was certainly beautiful, but he did not enthuse over her.

The Duchess, determined to keep him interested, had concentrated on amusing Mary-Lee.

A party had been specially given for her with a number of children of her own age.

Because Mary-Lee was to go to the Country, the entertainment had taken place before luncheon.

There had been a "Punch and Judy" Show and a Magician.

The children had then all found presents on their plates in the Dining-Room.

Roby thought now that Patrick, who had arranged everything, was getting little thanks for it.

"I will go and see if there is any sign of her," Patrick said, and walked from the Drawing-Room.

"You certainly have a very fine house," Clint Wickham said when he and Roby were alone.

"I am extremely grateful to you for restoring it to how it looked when it was first built," Roby replied.

He laughed before he added:

"That is, of course, with the exception of ten bathrooms, which I am sure would have made my Great-Grandfather's hair stand on end!"

"Only ten?" Clint Wickham asked. "I should have thought we would need more than that!"

"They can be added later," Roby said quickly, "and I assure you it has been a Herculean feat to achieve what is already there."

"To-morrow you must show me round the Estate," Clint Wickham said as if he were not listening to what Roby was saying.

"Yes, of course," Roby agreed. "And I had the idea you might like to build a small race-course."

He paused, and as Clint Wickham did not speak, he went on:

"I saw you were interested last night when Lord Burnham was discussing his. There is a place beyond the paddocks which is flat. Your horses would certainly appreciate it."

"Patrick told me you had bought some thorough-breds," Clint Wickham said, "and I am looking forward to seeing them."

"Personally, I think they are magnificent," Roby replied, "but then, I am prejudiced!"

Then as if he suddenly remembered, he added:

"And, by the way, the Governess that Patrick and I have engaged for your daughter is a very good rider. I thought that was something you would expect so that she could accompany Mary-Lee when she went riding."

There was no time for Clint Wickham to reply because the door opened and Patrick exclaimed:

"She is here!"

Clint Wickham had taken only a few steps towards the door when a small girl came running into the room.

"Poppa! Poppa!" she cried. "I'm here!"

She put her arms out and Clint Wickham picked her up and swung her off her feet.

"I was getting worried in case you had lost your way," he said.

"We came very, very quickly!"

"You enjoyed the party?"

"Not really," Mary-Lee replied. "The children were stuffy and the Conjuror wasn't as good as the one we had in New York!"

Clint Wickham laughed.

"You are too young to be critical!"

He put Mary-Lee down on the floor and she looked up at him, her head on one side.

"What is qu-it-tal?" she asked.

"Someone who finds fault," her father answered.

"I said 'Thank you' very nicely, just like you told me to."

"That's my girl! Now come and have some tea, very English tea with an iced cake and hot scones."

"Hot stones?" Mary-Lee asked. "What are they?"

"They are Scottish buns," Roby explained before Clint Wickham could reply. "I can see your father is educating you in the right way!"

Mary-Lee was not listening.

She pulled off her bonnet and flung it down on a chair before inspecting the food that was arranged on a table in front of the sofa.

It was then that Patrick came into the room.

"I have arranged for the Warminsters' maid who came down from London with Mary-Lee," he said to Clint Wickham, "to have tea in the Housekeeper's Room. Then she will go back to London."

Clint Wickham looked at his daughter.

"Did you thank the woman who brought you here?" he asked.

"Not much," Mary-Lee admitted. "She was very dull and didn't tell me any stories about the places we were passing, like you do, Poppa."

"You cannot expect stories from everybody you meet!" Clint Wickham objected.

"Anyway, not from the English," Patrick remarked. "They have no imagination."

He grinned before he added:

"Not like the Irish!"

"They talk a lot," Roby chimed in, "but if Mary-Lee has any sense, he will bring up his daughter not to listen to the honeyed tongues of those who have 'kissed the Blarney Stone'!"

Both Patrick and Clint Wickham laughed.

Mary-Lee was not listening.

She was eating chocolate biscuits and iced cake, having refused the hot scones.

When the tea was finished, Clint Wickham said to his daughter:

"I think, young lady, we had better go and meet your Governess and see if your room is as comfortable as I expect it to be."

He glanced at Roby before he added:

"I was always brought up to believe that English

children were stuck away in attics so that they could be neither seen nor heard!"

"That is certainly untrue where I was concerned," Roby replied, "but come and see for yourself."

They walked up the beautiful carved staircase.

Mary-Lee held on to her father's hand, chattering about the journey from London.

"There were lots of little baby lambs in the fields," she said, "but we drove by so fast that I couldn't see them properly!"

"You will find plenty of baby lambs in the fields here," Roby said.

The money he had paid the farmers had made it possible for them to increase their livestock.

They had been abjectly grateful.

As they reached the School-Room, Roby hoped that Tila would be waiting for them.

He was not disappointed.

She was standing in the centre of the School-Room, looking, he thought, every inch the part.

She was wearing a plain navy blue dress with white collar and cuffs.

She had meant it to be austere.

Yet it seemed to throw into prominence her small, pouted face which was dominated by her deep blue eyes.

They were not the blue of a summer sky, but of a turbulent sea.

Her hair was fair, the gold of the rising sun.

Although she had pinned it neatly at the back of her head, she could not repress the small curls which softened the lines of her oval face.

As Clint Wickham walked into the room she looked at him in surprise.

He was not in the least what she expected.

If that was what she was thinking, it was exactly what he was thinking about her.

From the description of English Governesses which he had been given at one time or another, Tila was very different.

He had rather expected someone middle-aged and certainly a plain Old Maid without looks or personality.

Instead, here was a young girl who was certainly lovely, if not beautiful.

She was looking at him with an expression of surprise.

There was also, he thought, a touch of fear in her eyes.

Clint Wickham was exceedingly perceptive.

He had learned in a hard School how to judge a man not by what he said, but by what he was.

He also prided himself in being able to look deep into a man or woman's character, to be quite unmoved by the superficial facade they presented to the world.

As he moved forward, his eyes on Tila, he heard Roby say:

"This is Miss Stevens, who will, I am sure, be able to give your daughter a very English education and also teach her how to enjoy our English countryside."

"That is certainly what I want," Clint Wickham said, and held out his hand.

As he touched her, Tila was aware of strong, forceful vibrations.

They were different from anything she had felt from any other man.

He was also surprisingly good-looking, which she had not expected, and, because he was a Texan, he was taller than Roby or Patrick.

In fact he seemed to tower over them, and also to over-power the room.

For the first time since she had heard of him, she could understand why Patrick spoke of him with respect.

Perhaps he *was* capable of running several great businesses in America despite the fact that he was so young.

"This is my daughter, Mary-Lee," Clint Wickham was saying as he released Tila's hand.

She took Mary-Lee's, and the child said:

"Poppa says you are going to teach me to be English, but I'm American, and I don't want to be anything else!"

"That is quite right," Tila said, "and of course you are proud of your country, just as I am proud of mine, so we shall just have to find out which is the best."

Mary-Lee laughed.

"Will that be a lesson?"

"We will make a list of the best things we know," Tila said, "then you can show it to your father and he shall judge who wins."

"And he can give us a prize," Mary-Lee added, "that's a nice idea!"

She looked round the School-Room.

"This is a very pretty room, Poppa! I like the pink curtains and the big comfortable sofa!"

"That is certainly one point to England!" Clint Wickham said.

"It's not as big as my room back home!" Mary-Lee added quickly.

"Then that is a point in America's favour!"

The child gave a cry of delight.

"I like this game! I'll have to think of lots of things and you must give me a big, big prize!"

"You have to win it first," Clint Wickham said.

He looked at Tila.

She had the idea that she had passed the first test, even though it was unintentional.

"I will leave Mary-Lee with you now, Miss Stevens," he said. "We will have a talk later in the day. If not—to-morrow."

"Thank you," Tila replied.

She knew that while this had been happening, Roby had been watching her apprehensively.

Clint Wickham turned towards the door.

Tila gave her brother a smile which was meant to be re-assuring.

She had wanted to wink at him but thought Mary-Lee was sharp enough not to miss it.

Tila would have been less re-assured if she had heard the conversation as Clint Wickham and Roby walked down the stairs.

"Miss Stevens seems rather young," Clint Wickham observed.

"I think she is older than she looks," Roby said quickly. "She seems intelligent, and as your daughter

69

is so young, I felt she should have a young person with her."

"It is a responsible position," Clint Wickham insisted, "and I am determined that Mary-Lee shall be well-educated."

Roby smiled.

"I agree with you, and that is what all women should be. At the same time, as you very likely know, in this country, while the boys go to what we call a 'Public School,' then on to a University, their sisters are taught by some middle-aged woman who knows little more than they do!"

"I have heard that," Clint Wickham said, "and it is something I will not tolerate where Mary-Lee is concerned."

He spoke in a hard voice.

Roby realised that he might be finding the *débutantes* whom Patrick was producing for him as dull and ignorant as he did himself.

When he had first gone to London he had been asked to the smart Balls of the Season.

He thought then it was his duty to his hostess to dance with her *débutante* daughter.

She had been squeezed in amongst the fascinating, beautiful, and sophisticated women with whom he later spent his time.

As he dragged some gauche and obviously stupid girl round the dance-floor, he was determined not to be caught in the "Matrimonial Fish-Net."

He very quickly, duty or no duty, ignored unmarried girls at any party he attended.

Instead, he concentrated on the fascinating Beauties whom the Prince of Wales found so irresistible.

The reason why Tila had never heard about any of his love-affairs was simply because "Discretion" was the Password in Mayfair.

It was not Roby, but the "Siren" with whom he was involved who was careful not to break the rules.

They went down the stairs. Roby was not wondering whether it was Patrick or Clint Wickham who would be disappointed if his invasion of the Ducal families failed.

He was more apprehensive whether, after what he had said, Clint Wickham would dismiss Tila as unsuitable.

If that happened, it would be a disaster and his tenancy would come to an end.

Roby could only hope that Tila would not fail him.

He must tell her somehow that she must prove herself to be intelligent.

It was something he had always thought her to be.

Clint Wickham, however, might have other ideas.

chapter four

TILA awoke early.

Her first thought was that she had not seen Clint Wickham the previous night.

It had been a relief that he had not sent for her before dinner.

Then she heard that Roby and Patrick were dining with him.

It was unlikely, she thought, that he would have her down while they were there.

She waited in the School-Room until it was half-past-ten, then went to bed.

She was reading a book, and was finding it enthralling.

She had found it in a bookcase in the landing outside the School-Room.

She imagined it must have been used ages ago by one of their Governesses.

Perhaps her Mother had put it there after the School-Room was shut up because she and Roby were too old for it.

It was a book of the Middle Ages, a story of Knights and gallant deeds which kept her reading until it was nearly midnight.

Now when she woke up she felt that the Knights were still with her and in a way guiding her.

She realised it was only half-past-six.

But the sun was turning the garden to gold and she had a sudden longing to be on Kingfisher.

She crossed the passage and went into the School-Room.

She found to her surprise that Mary-Lee was there, standing at the window.

"You are early!" Tila exclaimed. "I thought as you had a long journey yesterday you would be tired."

"I'm not tired, and I want to go riding," Mary-Lee replied.

Tila had a sudden idea.

"Shall we go to the stables," she suggested, "and perhaps you would like to have a short ride before breakfast."

Mary-Lee jumped for joy.

"I'd like that. I'd like it very much!"

Then Tila stopped.

"I wonder if there is a pony for you to ride?"

She thought it was something which Roby perhaps would have forgotten to supply.

Mary-Lee laughed.

"Back at home I ride the big horses on Poppa's Ranch, and he said a pony is not good enough for me now."

It seemed surprising for a child not yet eight.

At the same time, Tila had always been told that

when Americans owned Ranches, the children rode as soon as they could walk.

She rang for Emily, who was astonished that they were up so early.

"I was bringin' yer breakfast at half-past-eight!" she said reproachfully.

"We will be back for it," Tila promised.

While Emily dressed Mary-Lee she ran to her own room to put on her riding-habit.

It was the one thing she had not had to buy because she could wear her Mother's.

As her Mother had hunted with her Father, she had gone to the smartest Tailor in London.

She had bought what at the time had been the most up-to-date riding-habit procurable.

She had hardly worn it before she died.

When Tila was old enough to wear it, she thought it was unnecessarily smart for her lonely rides on Kingfisher.

Because she was alone at Staverly Court, she could jump onto her horse's back in whatever she was wearing.

If she bridled and saddled Kingfisher early in the morning, he would follow her round the garden while she picked flowers.

If she was doing any of the other things she had to do, he was always available.

Now she thought it was the right moment for her to wear her riding-habit.

She would be properly attired as, of course, a Governess should be.

Her riding-habit accentuated her small waist, and

she wore a white muslin blouse underneath.

This had also belonged to her Mother.

She had an idea that within the last few years riding clothes had become even more austere.

But she comforted herself with the thought that no one would expect a Governess to be anything but out-of-date.

In actual fact she looked very smart as she returned to the School-Room.

Mary-Lee was ready and waiting for her.

The child was wearing a very pretty light riding-habit which Tila noted at once had a divided skirt.

She thought it was sensible in anyone so young.

At the same time, it would certainly cause a great deal of criticism if the neighbours saw her.

She was not, however, prepared to say anything at the moment.

Taking Mary-Lee by the hand, they hurried down a back staircase where no one would see them.

They left the house by a garden door which led towards the stables.

It was just past seven o'clock when they reached them.

A young groom was carrying a fresh pail of water into a stall.

"Go and choose a horse you think would suit you," Tila said to Mary-Lee.

She had already decided which one she wanted for herself when it had arrived from Tattersall's Sale Rooms.

It was a dark bay, very spirited, and had, she thought, a touch of Arab blood in it.

She told the groom to saddle the horse, and as he started to do so, Mary-Lee cried:

"I've found the one I want, Miss Stevens!"

Tila passed several stalls until she found the child patting a very beautiful chestnut.

She was sure it had been Roby's choice.

He had a passion for chestnuts, and this was a particularly fine specimen.

Seeing the way it was nuzzling against Mary-Lee and enjoying being made a fuss of, she thought that it would not be too obstreperous.

Five minutes later they were riding out of the stables.

Tila realised that Mary-Lee had not exaggerated when she said she could ride.

She was obviously completely at home in the saddle, although the groom had to shorten the stirrups considerably.

"I like this horse—I like it very much!" Mary-Lee was saying.

Tila was having a little trouble with her bay.

He was showing his independence by rearing and bucking, but not too maliciously.

They reached the flat land which was a little way from the house.

It then occurred to Tila that she should have had Mr. Wickham's permission before riding his horses.

Then she told herself she was not certain he would allow her to do so anyway.

Whatever happened, she would have had one ride on the finest animal she had ever seen.

She meant to take Mary-Lee very gently in case

the child was not as proficient a rider as she professed to be.

She need not have worried.

Mary-Lee galloped off ahead of her.

She moved so quickly that Tila had to urge her horse forward to catch up with her.

They galloped for a long way over ground in which Roby could not afford to sow a crop.

They drew in their horses only when a high fence loomed ahead.

"I want to jump that fence," Mary-Lee exclaimed.

There was a determination in her voice that told Tila it would be a mistake to forbid her to do so.

Instead, she said:

"I think we would be wise to take our horses easily and to get used to them before we start jumping."

She thought for a moment that Mary-Lee was going to defy her and added quickly:

"I have something to show you, something I think you will find very exciting."

"What is it?" Mary-Lee asked.

"Do you see that wood over there?" Tila asked, pointing it out. "That is a very secret wood, and I want you to ride through it."

"Secret? Why is it secret?" Mary-Lee asked.

"That is something I am going to tell you later," Tila answered, "but first you are going to tell me what you feel about it."

The child was intrigued, as Tila knew she would be.

They galloped towards the wood.

It was where Tila had gone almost every day on

Kingfisher, where she told herself stories which were part of her thoughts, her mind, and her happiness.

As they entered what was known as "Bluebell Wood" Tila said to Mary-Lee:

"I do not want you to talk, just follow me through the wood, then tell me afterwards what you saw, what you heard, and what you felt."

Mary-Lee looked at her enquiringly.

"Is it a game?"

"A very special game, and I will tell you all about it later. Now do exactly as I say."

She rode ahead, moving over the moss-covered, twisting paths between the trees.

As she did so, she found herself slipping into one of her daydreams.

They had been the only companions she had in the long months when Roby was away in London, when there was no one at Staverly except for the Coblins.

Now the sunshine gleamed golden between the trees.

There was the flutter of birds overhead, and she was caught up in the enchantment that never failed her.

In the centre of the wood there was a deep pool which, however hot the summer, never ran dry.

There were willow trees hanging over it.

As they came in sight, a moorhen followed by nearly ten small chicks hurried behind the bushes which overhung the water.

Tila paused for a moment by the pool, looking down into its dark water.

She wondered if the nymphs she was sure lived in

it were the water-nymphs who had tempted Hylas.

She did not speak, however, and they rode on.

Now there was a mass of bushes coming into blossom.

She and Mary-Lee had their first sight of the butterflies hovering over them.

There was the buzzing of bees as they collected nectar to make honey.

A moment later the whole wood seemed to be carpeted in blue.

It was here every year that the bluebells were breathtaking.

To Tila they were even lovelier than the garden flowers.

She drew in her horse to look at them and wondered if Mary-Lee was as moved as she was.

They were now on the edge of the wood.

There was a small stream for the horses to wade across before they were back on the flat land again.

Only when they were out in the sunshine did Tila look at Mary-Lee enquiringly.

As if she knew she could now speak, Mary-Lee exclaimed:

"It was lovely! Fairyland! I am sure there were fairies flying amongst the butterflies."

Tila smiled.

"That is what I have always thought."

"I saw the little baby ducks on the water."

"They were moorhens," Tila explained. "What did you think of the pool?"

"Is it a magic pool?" Mary-Lee asked.

"Very, very magical to me!" Tila smiled.

"Why?"

"Pools in woods are always magical," Tila replied. "But this one is special."

As they rode straight across a field she told her the story of Hylas.

The water-nymphs had lured him into the pool in which they lived so that they would never lose him.

Mary-Lee listened attentively.

"How did he breathe under water if he was a man?" she asked.

"I think the water-nymphs must have taught him how to do so," Tila replied.

There was silence. Then Mary-Lee said:

"I 'spect Poppa would think he was drowned."

"You are not to spoil my story!" Tila said. "I like to think he is still there, swimming with the nymphs as the mermaids do in the sea."

There was silence as they rode on.

Then Mary-Lee said:

"Poppa says there's no such thing as fairies."

Tila thought scornfully that was just the sort of thing an American Businessman would say to a child.

"I believe in fairies," she said, "but, of course, they will not appear to people who do not believe in them."

"If I believe in them, will I see them?" Mary-Lee enquired.

Tila nodded.

"We do not always see things with our eyes," she said, "but we know they are there, and your heart tells you what is true and what is false."

"I want to see them," Mary-Lee said firmly.

"Secret things vanish when you expect everything to be like a stone you can hold in your hand," Tila said. "Have you heard of 'Fairy Gold'?"

Mary-Lee thought for a moment.

"I don't think so."

Tila told her how Fairy Gold could be seen, but vanished if you tried to touch it.

Mary-Lee thought this was funny and laughed.

"Poppa wouldn't like that. He has lots and lots of gold, and if it vanished, he'd be very angry!"

"With Fairy Gold we can buy the things we have been talking about this morning—the water-nymphs in the pool, the fairies, the butterflies, and, of course, the goblins who live under the trees."

Mary-Lee was excited by this.

"Tell me about the goblins," she begged.

Tila told her what she had believed ever since she was small, that there were goblins working under the trees, who came out at night.

She also told her about the fairies who danced and left a circle of toadstools among the grass.

Mary-Lee was thrilled.

"Show me one—show me one!" she cried.

They rode to where Tila knew there were always mushrooms in one particular field.

She had often picked them for Mrs. Coblin to cook.

She found some and they appeared to be in a circle.

Mary-Lee believed them to be toadstools left by the fairies.

"I do not think these came here last night," Tila

said. "I am sure we shall find some better circles when we go walking in the woods."

"Tell me more stories about the fairies," Mary-Lee pleaded.

"I think we should go back for breakfast now," Tila said, "but perhaps we could go riding again later on this morning. I will take you to another wood which is full of fir trees. I am sure we shall find lots of exciting things there!"

"It has been very exciting this morning," Mary-Lee said.

As she spoke, just ahead of them they saw somebody on a horse.

"There's Poppa!" Mary-Lee exclaimed.

She urged her horse forward and, as she hurried towards her father, Tila followed.

She had not expected Mr. Wickham to ride before breakfast.

She was almost sure that Roby and Patrick had stayed at Staverly last night.

Therefore, she thought they would take him to see other parts of the Estate where Roby had started to make improvements.

"As Wickham is paying," he had said to Tila, "I can do so many things I have always wanted to do but never had the money."

"Do be careful!" she warned. "Supposing, having paid so much for the house, he resents contributing to the land?"

"I cannot believe he expects to live like a King while all around him the land is going to rack and ruin!"

He spoke so positively that Tila did not go on arguing.

At the same time, she thought it would be wiser of Roby to explain what he was doing.

It would be a mistake to let the expenses come in later as a surprise.

She was worried in case they had to pay for the land improvements themselves out of what they would receive in rent.

Then she was determined to save.

They would need every penny when Mr. Wickham returned to America.

Otherwise they would have no money to keep up the house, glorious though it might be.

Mary-Lee had reached her father.

As Tila approached more slowly, she could hear the child telling him excitedly how much she had enjoyed the ride.

Tila joined them, and Clint Wickham, giving her what she thought was a hard look, said:

"I was not expecting you to go riding so early in the morning, Miss Stevens."

"I am sorry if we have done anything wrong," Tila replied, "but Mary-Lee and I were both awake, and it was such a lovely morning that I thought we should go for a short ride before breakfast."

"It is now a quarter-to-nine," Mr. Wickham said, "and when I heard that you had gone I thought perhaps you might be in some difficulty."

He spoke in a pointed manner, Tila thought.

It was as if he were implying that it was she who would be in difficulty, and not Mary-Lee.

She thought it would be a mistake to argue with him.

Mary-Lee fortunately interposed by saying:

"I like this horse, Poppa, I like it very much!"

"I think it might be too big for you," Mr. Wickham remarked, as if he were determined to find fault.

He was riding a large black stallion, which was one Tila had guessed he would like.

It would have been her own second choice, if she had not ridden the bay.

"Now I am hungry for breakfast," Mary-Lee said. "I'll race you, Poppa, back to the stables."

She set off as she spoke.

Tila had to admit that she rode with an expertise and an ease that she would not have expected even from an English child.

Clint Wickham followed Mary-Lee, and Tila could see he rode exceptionally well.

He looked, like her Father had, as if he were part of his horse.

She followed at a respectful distance, as, she thought with a smile, befitted an employee.

When she reached the stables the grooms were waiting to take their horses.

Mr. Wickham watched Tila as she dismounted, then he said:

"I have appointments this morning, Miss Stevens, and I suggest that you give Mary-Lee her lessons, then I will let you know what are my plans for this afternoon."

He did not wait for Tila to answer, but merely turned and walked away into the house.

Mary-Lee was patting her horse.

When he was taken to his stall she slipped her hand into Tila's.

"That was fun!" she said. "I want to ride again after breakfast and not have those horrible lessons Poppa was talking about."

"You will have to do your lessons as your father said," Tila replied, "but we will have a very special one."

"What is a very special lesson?" Mary-Lee asked suspiciously.

"One that you will enjoy, and so shall I," Tila replied.

They went up to the School-Room.

While they were having breakfast Tila was hoping she would have a chance to see Roby.

She had expected him to go back to London with Patrick yesterday evening.

They might, however, have stayed at the Dower House.

If they had done that, and she hoped they had not, it would have been a mistake.

The less Clint Wickham knew about the Dower House, the better, although there was no reason that he should connect her with it in any way.

When breakfast was over, Mary-Lee looked at Tila suspiciously.

"What are we going to do now?" she asked.

"I thought we would have a History lesson," Tila replied.

Mary-Lee groaned.

"I hate History, but Poppa says I have to learn about it."

"This lesson is a very special one," Tila said. "We are going to explore the house, and there is a lovely story to be found in every room."

"A story?"

There was a cry of delight, then Mary-Lee was jumping about beside her.

Because Tila was frightened of running into Mr. Wickham, they started at the top of the house.

They went first to the roof, then worked their way down.

Because she knew the history of every stick and stone, she was sure that Mary-Lee would be entranced.

She was, from the moment they climbed out onto the roof.

First, as Tila knew, there was a glorious panoramic view of the countryside.

Then there were the statues with which the roof was ornamented, as well as the flag-pole, although the Staverly standard was not flying.

Tila explained to Mary-Lee that the standard, which Roby had replaced with a new one, was flown only when the Head of the Family was in residence.

"Why cannot Poppa fly it?" she wanted to know.

"He can fly only his own standard, and as he is an American, I imagine he does not have one," Tila answered.

She thought as she spoke that perhaps that was another thing Clint Wickham wanted with his "Dynasty."

He would incorporate his own meagre quartering with those of his Ducal bride.

She would doubtless have a large number.

That way, she thought scornfully, if nothing else, he would have his name in *Debrett's Peerage*.

Tila and Mary-Lee spent so long on the roof that by luncheontime they had only just descended from the attics to the Third Floor.

"I want to see it all, every bit of it," Mary-Lee cried, "and you promised me a story in every room!"

"Every room, every picture, and every book," Tila exclaimed.

She had expected that Mary-Lee would be asked down to luncheon with her father.

However, she was informed by the footman who looked after the School-Room that Mr. Wickham was out for that meal.

Tila was delighted, but of course Mary-Lee was disappointed.

Because she had no orders to the contrary, she and Mary-Lee went riding again in the afternoon, but only for little more than an hour in case the child should be tired.

Tila rode another horse as spectacular as the one she had ridden in the mornning.

But she could not help feeling that she was being disloyal to Kingfisher.

At the same time, it was a joy to have something so young and spirited beneath her.

She was in fact prepared to risk anything, even Mr. Wickham's wrath.

They were just starting tea in the School-Room when a message came upstairs to say that Mr. Wickham had returned.

He wanted his daughter to join him.

Mary-Lee was looking very attractive in a lace-trimmed dress with a blue sash.

"Go downstairs to your father," Tila said.

"Aren't you coming too?"

"No, dear, he wants you. I shall be here when it is time for you to go to bed."

For a moment Mary-Lee pouted.

"I want you to come and tell Poppa what an exciting day we've had."

"I am sure you will tell him that without me," Tila argued.

To her surprise, Mary-Lee put her arms around her waist and hugged her.

"It's been a lovely day," she said, "the loveliest day I have ever had!"

Then she ran across the room and disappeared down the stairs.

With a wry smile Tila looked across to the window to look out.

She, too, had enjoyed the day.

Yet she was almost certain that Clint Wickham would not approve of the way in which she was teaching his daughter.

'He is hard and materialistic,' she thought.

She was sure what he wanted was exercise-books filled with sums.

She had always hated arithmetic when she was a child.

He would also want books filled laboriously with verbs and adjectives.

Besides grammar, there would be essays which

were inevitably boring because they took such a long time to write.

She sighed.

She told herself that if she did not do what Mr. Wickham expected, he might dismiss her.

She was sure of this when Mary-Lee came back two hours later.

"Did your father tell you what he has been doing?" Tila could not help asking.

She was curious, and she also wanted to know where Roby was and if he had gone back to London.

"He went to see a Farm," Mary-Lee answered surprisingly.

"Why did he do that?" Tila asked.

"It was a 'Model Farm,' " Mary-Lee explained, "and now Poppa wants to have one like it!"

Tila understood.

Roby was tempting him to improve the farms on the Estate.

Of course these were out of date and badly stocked.

It was clever of him to show Clint Wickham a model farm.

She knew to whom it belonged.

It was quite obvious what Roby and Patrick had planned.

Roby could have a modern farm on his Estate and Patrick would get his usual rake-off on everything that was spent.

It struck her that both men were behaving if not crookedly, then greedily.

"But," she asked herself, "why not?"

If Mr. Wickham wanted the best and for his own ulterior motives, then he must be prepared to pay for it.

She was quite sure in her own mind that was the reason for making Staverly look as it did. The house, the gardens, the Park, and now the farms would impress the girl he wished to marry.

He intended to give himself a good "background" before he actually proposed.

For the first time, she wondered why Patrick had not made him buy a house.

Then she knew without asking the question that it would be very difficult to find one as impressive as Staverly.

If a similar house belonged to an aristocratic family, everything would, of course, be entailed.

But Patrick had been very clever.

Staverly was outstanding, even amongst the stately houses of England.

It would certainly make Mr. Wickham the right "backdrop" for the performance of becoming the Bridegroom of one of the most blue-blooded young women in the land.

"Good luck to him!" she told herself.

Then, because she was still curious, she asked Mary-Lee:

"Was your father alone?"

"Yes, his friends have gone away," Mary-Lee replied. "They told me I was very pretty, Miss Stevens. Do you think I'm pretty?"

"You are very pretty when you smile, and rather ugly when you look cross!" Tila replied.

Mary-Lee laughed.

"When do I look cross?"

"When you cannot get your own way."

Mary-Lee ran to the mirror to examine her face.

"Now I am pretty!" she said. "And one of the men who was with Poppa thought you were pretty too, and Poppa said 'Too pretty to be a Governess!'"

Tila thought this was what she had expected.

She might as well hear the truth "out of the mouths of babes and sucklings" than wait for Mr. Wickham to dismiss her.

She helped Emily to put Mary-Lee to bed.

After she had heard her prayers the child put her arms round her neck and said:

"I love you, Miss Stevens, and I think you're very, very pretty!"

"Wait until I am cross with you," Tila answered, "then you will think I am ugly."

"Very, very ugly!" Mary-Lee laughed.

Tila kissed her good-night.

"Go to sleep," she said, "the Angels will be watching over you."

"And the fairies?"

"Of course!" Tila smiled. "And we might find some pictures of them in the Library. Shall we look to-morrow?"

"That will be exciting!" Mary-Lee exclaimed.

Tila went back into the School-Room.

She was just going to her own room when a footman came up the stairs.

"The Master asks if you'll go to the Study, Miss."

It was what Tila expected.

At the same time, her heart gave a little thump.

If she had to leave Staverly, she wondered what Roby would say about it—or, rather, it was Patrick who would be upset.

She took a quick glance at herself in the mirror to see that her hair was tidy.

Then she followed the waiting footman downstairs.

Because he assumed she would not know the way, he escorted her to the Study.

He opened the door to announce her.

As he did, Tila had a sudden longing to put back the clock and find her father sitting at the desk.

Her mother would be sewing in an arm-chair by the fire.

With an effort she forced herself now to remember that her name was "Stevens," not Staverly.

She was the Governess to the daughter of an American Millionaire.

Clint Wickham was standing at the window, looking out onto the garden.

She had reached the centre of the room before he turned.

He did not move directly towards Tila but stood looking at her.

He was taking in the fair curls round her forehead and the whiteness of her skin against the dark blue of her dress.

She felt sure he was thinking she was not what he wanted.

Without being aware of it, her chin lifted a little.

The expression of wariness which had been in her eyes now changed to one of defiance.

At last, after what seemed a long silence, Mr. Wickham moved towards her.

"I am afraid our talk, Miss Stevens, has been somewhat delayed."

He indicated a chair.

"Please, sit down."

Tila obeyed him, and he sat facing her.

"I have been hearing garbled tales from Mary-Lee," he began, "about her lessons to-day. She certainly enjoyed them. However, I am wondering if they are really practical."

"I think so," Tila replied politely.

"I would like to ask you," Mr. Wickham mused, "what you consider the most important possession my daughter has."

Tila had been expecting a trick question, and without hesitating she replied:

"Her imagination."

"Imagination?" Mr. Wickham replied. "Why do you say that?"

"Because it is the one thing in life which will ensure that whatever happens to her, she will never be alone."

Tila was really thinking of herself.

At the same time, she knew she had surprised Mr. Wickham, who was expecting a different answer.

"I fail to follow your reasoning," he said.

"If you think it out," Tila explained, "our imagination is the one thing which makes us different from the animals, and as it develops, we realise we can reach the stars."

She paused, then went on:

"We also find, whatever our circumstances may be, all the things that really matter in life, regardless of money."

Mr. Wickham sat back in his chair.

"You surprise me, Miss Stevens!" he admitted. "Have you thought this out by yourself?"

"With a question like that, one can speak only as one feels, and not in some impressionist, abstract manner."

Unexpectedly, he laughed.

Then, as if he felt he should explain, he said:

"I do not mean to be rude, but you look only a little older than Mary-Lee, and yet at the moment you are talking like a Doctor of Philosophy!"

"It was not my intention to try to impress you, Mr. Wickham," Tila answered, "merely to be honest, and I think from what Mary-Lee has said to-day you have deprived her of something more important in life than facts and figures."

"*I* have deprived her?" Clint Wickham questioned.

"Of course. You cannot tell her what you do not know yourself," Tila replied. "What you have learnt in perhaps a hard School is very different from what a child who lives in an over-comfortable, over-cushioned life can understand."

"Now, what do you mean by that?" Mr. Wickham asked.

Tila smiled, and it made her look very lovely.

"I am trying to explain why Mary-Lee needs, and I think it is very important, to use her imagination."

Mr. Wickham rose to his feet.

He walked across the room, then back again before he said:

"I asked you to come downstairs to see me, Miss Stevens, because I thought you were too young and too inexperienced to teach my daughter, who I wish to have a very comprehensive education."

"I thought that was what you were thinking," Tila murmured.

"You anticipated what I was going to say?" Mr. Wickham asked sharply.

"Yes."

"How could you do that?"

"Because of what you felt when you met me and because, I suppose, I know how your mind works."

"How can you possibly know that?" he asked.

Tila did not answer, and after a moment he said sharply:

"Answer my question!"

"Very well," Tila replied. "You are a Businessman, you are enormously rich, and at a young age you command, through your money, a position which a great many men all over the world would envy. It would be impossible, therefore, for you not to be tough and in a way hard."

She paused, wondering if she was "burning her boats" completely before she went on:

"But that is not what you want for your daughter who, to begin with, is a child and, secondly, will be a woman."

Clint Wickham was staring at her, but he did not speak.

After a moment Tila went on:

"Facts and figures are important for a boy, but they are not going to make Mary-Lee charming, delightful, and a very attractive woman."

She paused, and then continued:

"It is what she *feels* and to what she can aspire which matters far more than if she knows what she can buy with a million pounds."

Her voice was very alluring as she said gently:

"All the money in the world cannot buy a woman's soft, sweet personality, nor can academic knowledge change her heart."

Tila was not quite certain what she was saying, or why she was saying it.

She only knew the words seemed to come to her lips.

They were true because they came from her heart and not from her brain.

That should have told her to keep quiet and impress Mr. Wickham with her ability to teach.

But she had said what she believed.

If he dismissed her for saying it, there was nothing she could do.

Then she realised he was staring at her with an expression of astonishment.

She waited, and after a moment he moved to sit down beside her.

Then he said in a very different tone of voice from the one he had used before:

"How, at your age, looking like you do, can you possibly speak like that?"

chapter five

WHEN Tila went up to bed it was nearly midnight.

She thought it was the most extraordinary evening she had ever spent.

After Clint Wickham had talked to her in the Study he had said unexpectedly:

"I am now going to dress for dinner, and I want you to dine with me."

Tila looked at him in surprise.

"Dine . . . with . . . you?"

"At eight o'clock."

She did not answer, and after a moment he said:

"Are you going to tell me that you have no wish to do so?"

"I . . . I would . . . like to," Tila replied honestly, "but it . . . would be a . . . mistake."

"Why?"

The question was abrupt.

Tila knew it would be unconventional as herself to dine alone with a man, but she was his employee, and that made it worse.

The servants would talk.

After a moment she said:

"In England a Governess may come down to luncheon but not to have dinner in the Dining-Room. To dine alone with her employer would be considered scandalous."

Clint Wickham laughed.

"It is what I would expect in England, but I am an American, and as you may know, we have no class in my country."

"Instead, money creates the barriers which we make with breeding," Tila replied.

"That is not an argument I wish to pursue with you," Clint Wickham replied, "and whether we are in England or Honolulu, I want you to dine with me."

"Very . . . well," Tila said, a little ungraciously, "I can hardly . . . refuse to obey . . . you."

She went from the Study, aware that his eyes were following her as she shut the door.

She ran up the stairs.

When she reached her room she asked herself if anything could be more unusual and fascinating than to argue as she had been doing with a man as clever as Clint Wickham.

She put on one of her pretty new evening-gowns.

It was certainly not as smart as anything the ladies whom Patrick had introduced to Mr. Wickham would be wearing.

She looked in the mirror.

Because it was a long time since she had been well-dressed, she thought that she looked "pretty."

She was sure it was Patrick who had said so,

but not because he particularly wanted to pay her a compliment when she was not there.

It was, she felt, to ascertain what was Clint Wickham's opinion of her.

"He nearly got me dismissed," she told herself resentfully.

After the talk she had just had with Clint Wickham, and because he had asked her to dinner, that now seemed unlikely.

Still, she could not be sure.

When she went downstairs, feeling a little shy, he was waiting for her in the Drawing-Room.

As she walked towards him she knew he was appraising her.

His eyes were as penetrating as they had been the first time they met.

He looked very smart in his evening-clothes and she knew, as they were very English, he must have bought them in Savile Row.

"Patrick will have got a rake-off on them!" she told herself.

Then she tried not to remember how both Patrick and her brother were exploiting Clint Wickham because he was so rich.

"It is what he deserves," she tried to tell herself.

Yet she knew as dinner progressed that she was being almost hypnotised by his knowledge.

She knew he was the cleverest man she had ever talked to.

At the same time, he was interested in what she had to say.

They argued about so many different things that Tila forgot what she was eating.

She found herself expounding theories of which she had always thought she was ignorant.

She knew, as she spoke, however, that they came from the many books she had read.

They had remained in her mind while she had never had a chance of expressing them.

Now they seemed to flow out smoothly through her lips.

It was with delight she was aware that Clint Wickham was racking his brain to duel with her verbally.

After dinner was finished they sat at the candle-lit table for a long time.

They were still arguing over first one subject then another.

It was difficult to focus on Mary-Lee's education.

What it really was, Tila thought later, was an expression of their own beliefs.

More than once Clint Wickham asked:

"How can you talk like this? How can you know so much? Who were your teachers?"

Tila laughed.

"I can answer the last question quite easily."

"Tell me," he said.

"Books, flowers, woods, horses," she replied, "and my imagination, in which I roam the world I have never been privileged to see."

He sat back in his chair.

"All I can say, Miss Stevens, is that you are a very remarkable young woman. I am rather frightened at what you will become by the time you are thirty."

"Why frightened?" Tila asked.

"It seems to me it will be a choice between a Professor at a University, or perhaps the first woman Prime Minister of England."

Tila laughed.

"That is very unlikely."

"And so are you, and therefore anything might be possible."

"That is what I should apply to you," she retorted, "with your material ambitions."

It was a provocative challenge, and once again they were arguing.

They continued it in the Drawing-Room, until suddenly Tila looked at the clock in astonishment.

"I must go to bed!" she said.

Clint Wickham rose.

"I find it hard to let you go," he said, "there is so much more I want to know."

"There is always to-morrow."

"I have a house-party arriving in the evening," he replied. "I wish now I had stayed here alone."

He paused before he added:

"Except, of course, for you and Mary-Lee."

"I am sure your house-party is of the utmost importance."

Tila knew that if Patrick had arranged it, the guests would include a Duke's daughter.

The rest of the party would doubtless consist of sophisticated, amusing married women, with or without their husbands.

They would entertain Clint Wickham when he returned to London.

Because he was so rich, he would move in the very best circles, besides being *persona grata* at Marlborough House.

She thought that with all that to enjoy, Clint Wickham was being hypocritical in saying he liked to talk to her.

Or perhaps while she was not aware of it, he was mocking her.

"Good-night, Mr. Wickham," she said, and moved towards the door.

She was aware as she did so that he had not moved from where he was standing.

He was just watching her go.

As she reached her bed-room, she went to the window.

She pulled back the curtains and looked out over the garden.

The fountain was still playing.

Now the rays of the water were not iridescent in the sunshine, but in the moonlight.

It made everything seem romantic and mysterious.

As always when she saw beauty, Tila felt it move into her heart and become a part of herself.

"How can I explain that to somebody like Clint Wickham?" she asked herself.

She undressed slowly, looking into the garden as she did so.

She put on her nightgown.

Then she took the pins out of her long hair and

brushed it, still watching the fountain.

She was lost in a world of fantasy that was more real than what was occurring at the moment at Staverly.

At last with a little sigh she put down the hairbrush.

Leaving the curtains still drawn back, she got into bed.

The light would wake her early, and perhaps once again she and Mary-Lee could ride before breakfast.

She had just shut her eyes when the door opened.

It flashed through her mind that it was Mary-Lee, and perhaps something was wrong.

Then, as she sat up, Clint Wickham came into the room.

He was carrying a candle in his hand.

It was unnecessary because the moonlight gave sufficient light.

She saw he was wearing a long, dark robe and she supposed that he had undressed, as she had.

"What is . . . it?" she asked. "What is . . . wrong?"

He shut the door carefully behind him, and walked towards her to set the candle down on her bedside table.

"What . . . has . . . happened? Why have you . . . come up . . . here?" she asked.

He sat down on the side of the mattress and said quietly:

"Nothing is wrong, but when you had gone, I knew I could not let you go."

"I . . . I do not . . . understand," Tila said. "You have . . . not told me to leave. I thought . . . you

105

would let me . . . stay and go on . . . looking after . . . Mary-Lee."

Clint Wickham smiled.

It crossed Tila's mind that the moonlight softened his face and he looked very handsome.

"I have come," he answered, "because I wanted to talk to you about ourselves."

"That . . . is a . . . mistake!" Tila said. "If anyone . . . realises you are . . . here they . . . will be . . . very . . ."

She was going to say "shocked," then substituted "surprised."

"No one will know," he said soothingly, "except you. I want you to tell me, Tila, what you think about me."

Tila smiled.

"That is an easy question. I think you are the . . . cleverest man I have ever met . . . even while you . . . have a lot of strange . . . ideas with which . . . I do not . . . agree."

"I feel the same about you," Clint Wickham said, "except that you are the most beautiful person I have ever seen."

There was a note in his voice which made Tila feel shy.

"Please . . ." she said. "I think . . . you should go . . . away . . . though I . . . enjoy talking to you . . . and if you . . . decide to go back . . . to London with . . . your party, we can . . . talk another . . . time."

"I want to talk to you now," Clint Wickham said. "I want you, Tila, as I have never wanted a woman in my life before."

She looked at him in sheer astonishment.

Now his voice was very deep.

She had a feeling, although he had not moved, that he was drawing nearer and nearer to her.

"I . . . I do not know . . . what you are . . . saying," she murmured a little incoherently.

"You are very young, and perhaps very innocent," he said, "but I want you to be mine, and I want to look after you. I promise I will do that."

Tila stared at him.

She could hardly believe this was happening, that Clint Wickham, of all people, was sitting on her bed.

He was also saying things that for the moment seemed quite incomprehensible.

As if he understood her confusion, he went on:

"What I want, Tila, is for you to belong to me. I want to teach you about love, and make sure you never again have to earn your own living."

Tila thought that although it seemed extraordinary, in some round-about way he was asking her to marry him.

He was waiting for her answer, and she stammered:

"B-but you . . . came to England to . . . marry a Duke's daughter!"

"So you have been told that," he said. "Yes, it is true. I have not had a chance to tell you why that is what I am going to do. My Mother was English and the English side of me has always wanted to be in England."

Tila was listening, but she felt he did not answer her question.

"If you . . . marry a Duke's daughter," she said, "why should you . . . talk to . . . me in this . . . strange . . . manner?"

"I am trying to explain to you," Clint Wickham said, "that I need you in a very different way."

He paused for a moment before he said:

"When I saw you in the School-Room, I knew you were different from any other woman I have ever seen. But I am also frightened by the effect you have on me!"

"Frightened?" Tila asked.

"The feelings I have for you," Clint Wickham went on, "are what I have never felt before, although I have met hundreds of women in one way or another."

"How can . . . you say this?" Tila asked. "I thought in fact you were somewhat . . . antagonistic."

"I told you I was frightened," he said, "frightened because I have always had complete control over my feelings, and they never surprised me until then."

Tila was still looking at him questioningly as he said:

"I knew to-night that you are exactly what I want in my life—someone to oppose me, stimulate me, and, if you like, inspire me."

His lips twisted for a moment before he said:

"That is a word I have never used to anyone—man or woman!"

"I would . . . like to do . . . that," Tila said. "At the same time . . . it is what . . . your wife will . . . want to do for you and doubtless . . . resent you relying on . . . anybody else."

"My wife has not yet been chosen," Clint Wickham said, "but she is in a very different position."

Tila looked away from him.

"Of . . . course!" she said coldly.

"Not the way you are thinking," Clint Wickham said quickly. "She will bear my name and in time my children, and I shall be important in this country as well as in America."

There was now a note of determination in his voice which told Tila he had it all planned.

It was a business deal, an operation which came from his brain and had nothing to do with his heart.

"I see you . . . have it all worked . . . out," she said. "And I really . . . cannot think . . . where I come . . . into it."

Clint Wickham smiled.

"You are so brilliantly clever, my dear, in some ways," he said, "and such a child in others."

Tila's eyes in the moonlight were very wide as she looked at him.

"What I am asking you," he said gently, "is to live with me and belong to me, and to help me as no one but you can do."

Again there was that mocking note in his voice as he said:

"I have never asked anyone to help me until now."

"To . . . live with . . . you?"

The words seemed to come jerkily from between Tila's lips.

Then she gave a startled cry.

"You are . . . not saying . . . you cannot . . . mean . . . ?"

She stopped and put up her hands to her breast, as if to protect herself.

Her voice, while almost incoherent, had a shocked note in it.

It would have been impossible for Clint Wickham not to recognise the horror in her eyes.

"I do not want to upset you," he said, "but I want you to understand how happy I could make you. You would be rich, my Precious, so rich that if we ever left each other, which I cannot believe is likely, you will never have to worry about money again! It will obtain everything you want."

As he finished speaking he realised that Tila had not moved and she seemed to be turned to stone.

Because he realised he had really upset her, he put out his hand towards her.

She gave a cry and shrank away from him.

"No . . . no!" she cried. "How can you . . . ask me to do anything so . . . wrong . . . so wicked? Mama would . . . have been h-horrified!"

Clint Wickham did not move, and she went on:

"Go away . . . please go . . . away and . . . forget that you ever . . . said anything . . . like that . . . to me!"

She drew in her breath.

"I . . . I ought to . . . leave here . . . I ought to get up and . . . go away . . . now!"

"Listen to me, Tila," Clint Wickham said. "I had no intention of upsetting you like this. I can only ask you to forgive me. I had no idea you would be shocked. Just put it down to the fact that I am an American and do not know how to behave!"

Tila did not answer, and he said after a moment:

"Please forget I ever came here. I can only tell you in all sincerity that I did not think you would be shocked."

"It is . . . wicked . . . a sin!" Tila said as if she must make him understand.

"It would be to you," Clint Wickham said. "So, please, Tila, please forgive me, and I swear to you I will never insult you in the same way again."

There were tears in Tila's eyes, but she tried to look at him.

Clint Wickham took a handkerchief from the pocket of his robe and, bending forward, wiped them away very gently.

"I am sorry—so very sorry," he said. "You cannot be so cruel as not to forgive me!"

"I . . . want to," Tila murmured, "but . . ."

As she spoke she was thinking she ought to leave.

Clint Wickham must have read her thoughts.

"If you run away now," he said, "I shall run after you! The house-party will find no host when they arrive to-morrow, and that will cause a terrible commotion!"

Tila knew he was trying to make her smile.

But her eyes were wary as she said:

"Promise me you will never again say anything like that to me."

"I promise!" Clint Wickham said. "But you must promise to stay and look after Mary-Lee and, incidentally, me!"

He saw the suspicion in the quick glance she gave him, and added:

"Not in the way I suggested, but the way we were to-night, talking, laughing, and arguing with each other, with you giving me new ideas and, as I have said before, inspiration. And that is something I have never had from anybody else."

"Is that what you really . . . want?" Tila asked.

It was the question of a child who was afraid of the dark, and Clint Wickham said:

"All I know is that I cannot lose you. As long as you stay you can make the rules and I will obey them, if it is possible for me to do so."

He took her hand in both of his, and because he was touching her he felt Tila quiver.

"There is something very precious between us," he said, "and surely you are intelligent enough to realise we cannot lose it?"

She was silent and he said:

"I want more than I have ever wanted anything in my whole life to kiss you, but because I am behaving as you wish me to do, I will just say good-night."

He bent his head as he spoke and kissed the back of her hand.

She felt his lips at first rather hard against her skin, then soft and somehow beseeching.

It gave her a strange feeling in her breast that she had never felt before.

"Good-night, my darling," Clint Wickham said, "and may God look after you as you will not allow me to do."

He rose as he spoke, picked up his candle, and walked towards the door.

As he opened it he looked back.

He thought for a moment, although, of course, it was a trick of the light, that two angels were standing like sentinels on either side of Tila's bed.

"You have shut the Gates of Heaven against me," he said, "and it is very lonely outside."

Then he was gone and Tila stared after him in bewilderment.

* * *

The next morning Tila was tired when she woke because she had not slept until the moonlight faded.

It was the calmness of the night before dawn breaks.

There was therefore no chance of her going riding before breakfast.

Mary-Lee was reproachful when she went to the School-Room.

"I thought you would come and wake me, Miss Stevens," she said.

"I am afraid I over-slept," Tila replied, "but we will ride immediately after breakfast, and there is another room I want to show you."

"With lots of stories in it?"

"Yes, lots of stories," Tila promised.

She thought as they went to the stables that it was more than likely Clint Wickham would have ridden before breakfast, as he had yesterday.

She found it hard to believe that what had happened last night had not been a dream.

Had he really come to her bed-room?

Had he sat on her bed in the moonlight and

asked her to be his mistress?

She found it hard to say the word even to herself.

She was not sure exactly what it implied.

She only knew from what she had read in the History Books that there had been mistresses as well as wives in the lives of Kings since the beginning of civilisation.

She had never thought very much about it until now.

Yet her books had told her that while a King's marriage was arranged for the good of his country, he chose his mistress because she meant something special to him.

The King gave them not a crown, but his heart.

She knew that was what every woman wanted in the man she loved.

But to belong to him without the blessing of the Church was wicked and a sin.

She remembered there being trouble in the village when one of the girls had come back from London.

She had been employed there and was expecting an illegitimate child.

Tila's mother had been told about it.

She had been horrified that such a thing should happen in a respectable family.

The girl had been shunned by everybody.

Finally she had committed suicide by throwing herself into the river.

Tila had not been very old at the time, but she

had heard it discussed by her Nanny and the house-maids.

The older women had said it was the best thing that could have happened to her.

Tila had thought them cruel and wished she had had a chance of saying something to the girl before she died.

She remembered now that she had not known exactly what was meant by an "illegitimate" baby. The village referred to it as a "bastard."

And it was something of which she was still ignorant.

She knew that if a man and a woman married, in the fullness of time they had children.

But how it occurred, she had no idea.

She only knew that if she allowed Clint Wickham to make love to her as he wanted to do, and if she lived with him, the same thing might happen to her.

Then she might be forced to take her own life by jumping in the river.

"How can I even think of such a thing?" she asked herself.

Then she remembered she had promised to try to forget what he had asked of her.

Even as she tried to do so, she remembered the feeling of his lips as he kissed her hand.

She thought, although she knew it was wrong, that perhaps it would be very wonderful if he kissed her lips.

Trying to forget her own feelings after what had

happened, she hurried Mary-Lee to the stables.

Once again they chose the horses they wanted to ride.

Tila asked for the one she had had first yesterday.

She wanted something that was spirited, something which would make her concentrate on what she was doing, and not remember Clint Wickham in the moonlight.

They galloped over the flat land.

They went into another wood, but to-day for Tila the magic was missing.

Instead of Hylas and the water-nymphs, she could only hear Clint Wickham's voice, see his eyes pleading with her.

With the greatest difficulty she tried to remember the stories of Knights and Dragons which would amuse Mary-Lee.

But the Knights as she described them looked like Clint Wickham.

The Princess he rescued who wanted to throw herself into his arms because she was so grateful to have escaped from the Dragon was herself.

The trouble was, Clint Wickham was also the Dragon.

"That was not a very good story!" Mary-Lee said to Tila's shame.

They rode back through the Park.

When they were walking their horses up the drive they suddenly came upon two men standing under one of the oak-trees.

Tila was aware that they were watching their approach.

As they drew nearer, they stepped out into their path and the two men came to their side.

"Hi!" one of them said. "Is that the Wickham gal you have with you?"

He spoke with a strong American accent.

As Tila looked at him she realised there was something about him she did not like.

She did not know why, but she sensed he was dangerous and she said, almost without thinking:

"No, it is not. It is the young lady who is staying with her."

"Is that so?" the American said with obvious disappointment in his voice.

Tila realised that Mary-Lee had turned her face to look at her.

In case the child should contradict what she had said, she remarked quickly:

"Come on! I will race you to the bridge!"

Mary-Lee needed no further encouragement.

She spurred her horse forward, and Tila followed.

Only when she had gone quite a distance did she turn round.

The two men were standing in the centre of the drive, talking to each other.

At the same time, they had turned their faces towards Staverly, as if they were discussing the house.

She was certain they were dangerous.

All the stories she had heard of kidnapping, especially of rich men's children, came back to her mind.

She knew she must not frighten Mary-Lee.

At the same time, she had to protect her from harm.

When they reached the stables, the grooms took their horses.

Tila deliberately led Mary-Lee through a back door so that they would not be seen if the men were still watching the front of the house.

They moved through the back corridors until they reached the hall.

"Go upstairs, dear," Tila said to Mary-Lee, "and ask Emily to help you change your clothes."

"Are you not coming with me?" Mary-Lee asked.

"I am going first to the Library to find a book I want to show you," Tila replied. "It is a very good story, and there are some lovely pictures in it."

There was no need to say any more.

"Hurry," Mary-Lee pleaded, "then perhaps I can hear the story before luncheon."

She went upstairs, and as soon as she was out of hearing, Tila said to a footman:

"Where is Mr. Wickham?"

"He's in t'Study, Miss."

He did not go ahead to open the door for her.

Tila hurried down the passage, hoping that Clint Wickham would be alone.

She listened outside the door for a moment, and

when she could hear no voices, she opened it and went in.

Clint Wickham was sitting at his desk, writing, and did not immediately look up.

Then, as if he sensed her presence, he saw she was there and rose to his feet.

She walked towards him, feeling suddenly too shy to meet his eyes.

"You look very lovely this morning!" he said in a low voice.

"I . . . I have . . . something to tell you."

She looked up as she spoke.

There was an expression of hope in his eyes which told her he thought she had changed her mind.

"It is about Mary-Lee," she said quickly. "I think she may be in danger!"

"In danger?" Clint Wickham exclaimed. "Why?"

"There were two Americans standing on the drive," Tila replied. "They asked me if Mary-Lee was your daughter."

"What did you tell them?"

"I told them she was a little girl staying with her."

Clint Wickham smiled.

"How, looking as you do, can you be so clever and so unerringly intelligent?"

"I . . . I am . . . frightened!" Tila said. "Perhaps they would have . . . kidnapped Mary-Lee!"

Clint Wickham looked angry, then he sighed:

"I thought here in England that those sort of things did not happen. She is well guarded when she is on the Ranch and in New York. The Ranch was patrolled day and night."

"These men might have . . . followed you . . . across the Atlantic," Tila said.

"There is always that possibility," Clint Wickham agreed. "It is one of the penalties for being rich!"

"What are . . . we to do . . . about Mary-Lee?"

" '*We*' is the right word," he said. "We are in this together, and, of course, you know I am relying on you."

"I will do . . . anything . . . you tell . . . me to . . . do," Tila replied.

Then she was afraid her words might be misconstrued, and added quickly:

"We . . . cannot have her . . . frightened."

"No, of course not," Clint Wickham agreed. "I will arrange to have the house guarded, and when you go riding you must take a groom with you, who will carry a revolver."

Tila nodded, then she said:

"I . . . I would like one too."

"You know how to shoot?" Clint Wickham asked.

"My father taught me when I was quite young."

He walked to the writing-desk and opened a drawer.

"This is one of my favourites," he said. "It was among my papers and I was surprised to see it in an English desk in an English house."

It was a small revolver, smaller than any gun Tila had seen before.

Clint Wickham gave it into her hand with a box of bullets.

"I can only hope that you never have to use it," he said.

"I hope so too," Tila replied in all honesty. "I cannot . . . imagine this . . . sort of thing happening . . . at Staverly."

"Neither can I," Clint Wickham said, "that is why I blame myself for not having taken precautions before now."

He sounded angry, and Tila said quickly:

"You must not . . . worry. It is very seldom anyone is . . . kidnapped in . . . England."

"I have no wish for my daughter to be the exception," Clint Wickham retorted, "and thank you, my lovely one, for warning me before any damage was done!"

The colour came into Tila's face at his words.

Then, as she saw the fire in Clint Wickham's eyes, she turned quickly away.

"I must . . . go and get ready for luncheon," she said.

"You are both having luncheon with me in the Dining-Room," he replied.

"No . . . I think . . . that would be a mis—" Tila began.

Then, as she saw the expression in his eyes, she remembered that to-night there would be a large party.

They might not see each other alone again until the weekend had passed.

"Very well," she said, "and we will not be late."

They were both smiling, and as their eyes met, it was somehow impossible for either of them to move.

Tila walked towards the door.

Then she was running down the corridor, running away from herself.

But holding the revolver in the pocket of her riding-habit as she did so.

chapter six

As they came back from their ride with the groom behind, Tila felt she had made a mistake.

There was really no reason to suppose that the two Americans she had spoken to on the drive were anything but tourists.

She now felt embarrassed that the groom was carrying a revolver.

The small one which Clint Wickham had given her was in the pocket of her riding-jacket.

"I was being over-dramatic!" she told herself.

At the same time, she felt her instinct could not be wrong.

Yet there was certainly no sign of the Americans on the drive, in the Park, or on the land over which they had galloped.

Because they had a groom with them, Tila did not go to her enchanted woods.

It was annoying to think that she was barred from them.

But, as she was riding a magnificent horse, she enjoyed herself.

It was impossible not to.

Mary-Lee had not been surprised at having somebody with them.

Only when they got back to the house did she say:

"I think it's more fun, Miss Stevens, when we go alone, and I like riding in the woods!"

"I know you do, dear," Tila replied, "but your Father thought we should be accompanied, at least for a little while."

Mary-Lee was not really interested.

By the time they reached the School-Room she was chatting away about what they would do that afternoon.

Tila had already learned from Emily that they were not expected down for luncheon.

She was rather surprised until she learnt that Patrick O'Kelly had arrived.

She reasoned that he had come in advance of the house-party to see that everything was ready for them.

She suspected that Roby would arrive later.

As Patrick was in the house, she thought it was wise of Clint Wickham not to have her and Mary-Lee to luncheon with him.

She had the idea that it would be very difficult for them not to show their feelings, and an Irishman could be very perceptive.

Then she told herself there was nothing to hide about *her* feelings, at any rate.

Yet she knew that was untrue.

She thought it would be impossible for her and Mary-Lee to go on exploring the house when all the guests had arrived.

It also looked like rain.

So she took Mary-Lee on the tour she had planned originally, starting at the cellars.

Mary-Lee was thrilled with the caverns which were underneath the house. They had been there since Elizabethan times.

Tila knew them well. She was, however, astounded when she saw the enormous number of bottles that were now in the racks.

She suspected that Patrick was responsible for them.

Of course they must have proved a very pleasant "rake-off" for him.

Having explored the cellars, they then went up to the Ground Floor.

They reached the Library.

Tila remembered where there was a number of Fairy-Tale books.

She found them one by one, and Mary-Lee was thrilled with every picture.

Some of the stories were those her mother had read to Tila when she was a little girl.

She put them on one side to take up to the School-Room.

"There are still some books I haven't seen!" the child protested.

"There are many more days, months, and years in which to do so," Tila replied.

Mary-Lee put her head on one side.

"Perhaps Poppa will go back to America. Back home on the Ranch I have no books like these."

"We will ask him to buy you some," Tila suggested, "or, perhaps, if you are very, very careful with these, you may borrow some of them."

"That will be nice, and you can read them to me," Mary-Lee answered.

Mary-Lee's words gave Tila a little jerk.

Was it possible that she would go to America with Clint Wickham and his daughter when they returned there?

As she thought about it, she knew it was something which would never happen.

If she did, even if he was not married, she had the feeling he would still be wooing her in his own way.

It would be very hard to prevent him from coming any closer.

What it really amounted to was that it was not a question of whether she would go to America.

It was whether she would be able to stay on at Staverly.

Everything within her cried out at the idea of her having to leave, perhaps never to see her home again.

Then she told herself she was being ridiculous.

How could she feel like this for a man she had only just met, a man who had insulted her?

Of course it was an insult what he suggested to her last night.

And yet because he had not touched her, except to

kiss her hand, she was not really angry with him.

"He is American and he does not understand," she said beneath her breath.

That was not the answer, and she knew it.

*   *   *

In the School-Room Emily changed Mary-Lee into one of her pretty and obviously very expensive dresses.

As she did so, she was chattering on about the party.

"There be twenty-six guests to dinner in th' Dinin'-Room," she said, "an' all th' best bed-rooms be ready for 'em."

It was with difficulty that Tila had not peeped over the bannisters to see them arriving, as Emily had done.

"Ever so smart, they be!" Emily went on. "Fevvers in their 'ats, an' diamonds in their ears."

"Did you learn any of their names?" Tila asked curiously.

"Only the Duchess 'as arrived," Emily replied. "The Duchess of Melchester I thinks 'er be."

Tila drew in her breath.

She knew a Duchess would be there.

She tried to prevent herself, but the words seemed to fall from her lips.

"Has Her Grace . . . brought a . . . daughter with . . . her?"

"Ow, yes, Miss! Lady Vivien Chester's 'er name, an' 'er's ever so pretty!"

That was the answer Tila had expected.

She tried to ignore the sudden constriction of her heart.

A footman brought a parcel to the School-Room, which was addressed to Mary-Lee.

"For me?" she asked excitedly. "What can it be, Miss Stevens?"

"I have no idea." Tila smiled. "Open it and see."

She thought it was from the house guests because it had not come by post and was tied up with ribbon.

Mary-Lee pulled the parcel open.

Inside was a small, very pretty musical-box.

She opened the lid and it played a tune, and she showed it to Tila excitedly.

Tila noticed that when the parcel was opened there was a note inside it.

When she picked it up, she saw it was addressed to her.

She knew then that the gift had come from Patrick.

She recognised his hand-writing.

Mary-Lee was playing with the box and opening and shutting the lid a dozen times.

Tila read the note. It was very short:

Dear Otila,
    This is a present for Mary-Lee. It is very
important that some delivery, however small,
is made immediately.

                                    Yours, Patrick

Tila stared at what he had written.

Then she knew that the present had just been a clever way of alerting her to her duties.

No one would be aware that he was communicating with her.

She had actually forgotten the condition to which she had agreed.

Because there had been so much else to think about, it had never occurred to her that she should have been spying on Clint Wickham.

That was what she had been told to do.

She felt a sudden revulsion at the thought of it.

She wanted to tell Patrick to leave her alone.

Then she remembered he had almost threatened her into agreeing to what he wanted.

He had hinted that the unknown person who had saved Staverly, Roby, and herself might be a very bad enemy.

'I have to find out something!' she thought dejectedly.

She was thinking what she should do, when another footman came to the School-Room to say:

"Mr. Wickham be expecting Miss Mary-Lee downstairs in th' Drawing-Room."

"Shall I take my box with me?" Mary-Lee asked.

"Yes, if you want to," Tila answered, "and remember to thank Mr. O'Kelly. He gave it to you."

"I will thank him very politely!" Mary-Lee smiled.

She looked up at Tila and added:

"Will you come with me and thank him too?"

"I think your Father would prefer to have you alone," Tila replied.

"He will not be alone with all those people there," Mary-Lee answered, "and they will make a fuss of me, just to please him."

Tila laughed.

She thought it amusing that the child was so intelligent as to realise that many of the compliments she was paid were really for her Father's benefit.

Aloud she said:

"Go down now and be very good and polite to everybody. If they pay you compliments, just say 'Thank you'!"

"I 'spect Poppa will do that," Mary-Lee said. "He likes hearing nice things about me."

"And so do I," Tila said as she smiled, "so remember to tell me about them when you come back."

"It would be more fun if you were coming with me," Mary-Lee answered.

She ran to the door, and the footman who was waiting outside followed her down the stairs.

Tila closed the books at which they had been looking.

Then she went to her own room.

She was thinking that the Duke's daughter whom Patrick had invited to Staverly would be dangled under Clint Wickham's nose.

Perhaps he would feel about Lady Vivien in the same way he had felt about her last night.

Then she told herself it was ridiculous to keep

thinking about him and what he had said.

She was shocked and she wanted to dismiss it from her mind.

The only possible excuse was that Clint Wickham was an American.

He therefore did not know how a Gentleman should behave.

She went to the window to look out at the fountain.

The sun was sinking in a blaze of glory and was reflected on the water spurting up towards the sky.

It was so incredibly lovely that she thought it became a part of herself, and her love for Staverly.

'Whatever happens, whatever he may say or does not say,' she thought, 'he has given us so much, so very much that we can never forget.'

*   *   *

After Mary-Lee had gone to bed, Emily gave Tila a glowing description of what the ladies were wearing at dinner.

Then Tila thought she would go to bed early.

She had undressed and was actually getting into bed when a thought occurred to her.

This would be a good night for trying to get some information for Patrick.

She lay back against her pillows.

She was trying to think of how she could find anything that would be of the slightest use to him.

She could not believe that anything that was very

revealing about Clint Wickham's affairs would be left lying about.

It would be locked up in a safe.

"I do not know what I am supposed to be looking for," she argued.

At the same time, there might be something, she supposed, in the drawers of the desk in the Study.

Perhaps even a letter-heading would be sufficiently revealing to those who would understand its significance.

'I suppose I shall have to look,' she thought grudgingly.

This would be a good evening to do so because the house-party would go to bed early.

She had learnt from Emily that to-morrow night there would be dancing to an Orchestra which was coming from London.

The party would therefore be very late going to bed.

To-night, after travelling by train and having been to parties and Balls during the week, they would want to retire early.

"If I wait until they are all in their rooms," Tila reasoned, "I can look through the desk, and if there is nothing there, then Patrick will just have to accept that I have failed."

She picked up a book which was by the side of her bed and started to read it.

She knew if she fell asleep she might easily not wake until dawn.

Then it would be too late.

She waited until her clock told her it was after one o'clock.

Because she was feeling sleepy, she decided not to wait any longer.

Accordingly, she got out of bed.

She picked up the dressing-gown which Emily had left ready for her on a chair.

It had belonged to her Mother and was very much prettier and more elaborate than anything she owned.

It had been her Mother's best and was of satin trimmed with little frills of lace.

Tila put it on and had turned towards the door before she hesitated.

Then she opened a drawer of her bedside table.

She took out the small revolver which Clint Wickham had given her.

She was quite certain she would not need to use it against anybody.

But she might be questioned as to why she had gone downstairs in the middle of the night.

If she was, she could say she thought she heard an intruder in the house and had gone to investigate, in which case, if Clint Wickham heard about it, he would expect her to take the revolver with her.

'I am being very sensible,' Tila told herself. 'I am prepared for any emergency.'

At the same time, she was praying that she would not be seen.

Because she knew the house so well, it was easy for her to make her way along corridors not in use.

They led across the centre block to descend by a narrow staircase to the Ground Floor.

It was, in fact, fortunate that she knew her way.

These stairs were not lit as the others were.

She was, however, guided by a nearly full moon.

The light coming through the windows made it easy for her not to slip on the narrow stairs.

She reached the Ground Floor in safety.

Now she was at the far end of the corridor and near the Library.

There were still a few lights left burning. Only every other sconce had been extinguished.

This meant, as Tila knew, that everybody had gone to bed, including Clint Wickham.

Swiftly and silently as a ghost she hurried to the Study door.

Opening it very carefully, she found, as she had expected, that the room was in darkness.

There was just a faint flicker of light from a dying fire.

Although it was warm in the daytime, it was still only April, and the nights were chilly.

A fire was lit in every room. It was easy for Tila to find a jar filled with spills on the mantelpiece.

She lit a candelabrum of three candles, which was on the desk.

It was a Regency table with brass ornamentation on the drawers, legs, and feet.

As she walked back to it, having thrown the spill into the fire, Tila felt as though her Father were sitting behind it, looking very handsome.

He was regarding ruefully the bills that were piled up in front of him and which he was unable to pay.

Then she told herself crossly that it was useless to dwell on the past.

Everything was changed, including this room and the desk itself.

'There must be something in the drawers,' she thought hopefully.

She was just about to pull one open when suddenly she heard a slight sound.

Everything had been so quiet and silent, almost as if the world had fallen asleep.

The sound made her start.

She stood still, listening.

Now there were other sounds, and she knew that somebody, or perhaps more than one person, was approaching the Study door.

She looked around her desperately for a place to hide.

Even as the door began to open, she fled towards the curtains that covered the windows.

She slipped behind them.

She was climbing as she did so onto the window-seat which was covered with the same crimson velvet as the curtains.

Her breath was coming quickly with fear.

For the moment she could only stand on the window-seat.

She felt the pumping of her heart must be heard by whoever had come into the room.

Then the door was shut and there was the sound

of footsteps, several of them, moving across the carpet.

"If y'know what's good for you, we won't waste any time!" an American voice said.

He spoke in a harsh nasal tone.

Tila put her hands on both the curtains in front of her and pulled them just a fraction apart.

She could not imagine what was happening.

Yet the American voice sounded somehow familiar.

She only dared to peep through the curtains with one eye, but it was enough.

What she saw was so horrifying that she felt not only her hands but her whole body was trembling.

Clint Wickham had been pushed into the chair behind the desk she had just left.

Standing on either side of him were two men.

She recognised the one who had spoken to her on the drive.

She saw now that he and the other man who had been with him were holding in their hands long sharp knives.

They glittered evilly in the candlelight.

"I tell you I have nothing here!" Clint Wickham said. "Anything that might be of interest to you is in London in my safe, or else in the hands of my Solicitors."

"If that's the truth," one of the men said, "you'll open the left-hand drawer of this desk with the key we found upstairs. If, as you say, there's nothin' there, you'll write a letter to your Solicitor tellin' him t' give us what we want."

"And while we're waitin'," the other man said, "you'll be put where nobody can find you."

He also spoke with an accent which proclaimed him to be an American.

"And if I refuse?" Clint Wickham asked. "Do you intend to kill me? In which case, I assure you, gentlemen, according to the Law of England, you will be hanged by your necks, which is a very unpleasant way of dying."

He spoke mockingly and with an ease which Tila could not help admiring.

It did not intimidate his two assailants, and they laughed jeeringly.

"No, we ain't gonna kill you, 'Mr. Moneybags,' we're too clever for that! But every time you refuse to do what we want, you'll feel the tip of this knife, and that'll hurt you more than it'll hurt us!"

He laughed at his own joke, and it was an evil sound.

Looking at him, Tila knew he was delighted that he had Clint Wickham, who was so important, in his power.

He wanted to torment and injure him.

Clint was wearing his white evening shirt and black trousers.

He must have removed his tie before they had appeared in his bed-room to threaten him.

Tila felt sure he had been the last person upstairs after his guests.

Because he was American and used to looking after himself, he had not rung for his Valet as her Father would have done.

The Americans must have got into the house earlier in the day.

It would have been easy for them to do so.

They would have hidden themselves somewhere in the Master Suite or otherwise found themselves a hiding place in a room no one was using.

It was unlikely Clint Wickham would have locked his door.

Now she could feel he was wondering what he could do, and she had to save him.

She had almost forgotten the revolver in her pocket.

Moving slowly in case she should be heard, she took her hand from the curtain.

She drew the revolver out of her dressing-gown pocket.

"Come on, we ain't got all night!" one of the men was saying impatiently. "Open the drawer or I'll do it m'self, an' knife you for causing me so much extra work!"

"There is nothing very interesting in it, if that is what you expect," Clint Wickham replied.

He picked up the bunch of keys the American had flung on the blotter.

Watching, Tila realised that because there was quite a number held by a gold key-ring the Americans had not used them themselves.

It would have taken too much time to find out which was the right one.

To put the key in the lock, Clint Wickham had to bend forward.

As he did so, the body of the man on his left-hand side was no longer partly concealed from Tila.

It was he who was the Ring-Leader, and as Clint Wickham moved he raised his knife menacingly.

She knew instinctively from the expression on his face that he was considering if he should plunge it into his back.

As she could feel the evil vibrating from him, she raised the revolver.

Her Father had taught her to shoot accurately.

It would be a mistake and undoubtedly cause a scandal if she killed a man.

She therefore aimed just below the wrist of the hand in which he held the knife.

Clint Wickham inserted the key in the lock.

As he did so, Tila fired.

The explosion seemed almost ear-shattering.

The American gave a scream of pain and fell backwards.

As his accomplice stared at him in astonishment, Clint Wickham acted.

He sprang from the chair in which he was sitting and knocked the man on his right backwards onto the floor.

The man fell to the ground with a thud and his knife dropped from his hand.

Clint Wickham picked it up, and, stepping over his prostrate body, went to the window.

"Give me the revolver," he said in a low voice, "and stay exactly where you are!"

Tila pushed the revolver through the curtains, and he took it from her.

Even as he did so, the door of the Study was thrown open.

The Night-Footman followed by the Night-Watchman, who was an elderly man, rushed into the room.

The American Tila had shot was lying on the floor groaning and clutching his shattered wrist.

The knife with which he had threatened Clint Wickham was quite a distance from him.

"Wot be 'appenin' 'ere, Sir?" the Night-Watchman asked. "We 'eards a shot!"

"These men were threatening me," Clint Wickham said, pointing to the American who was bleeding.

"This is turrible, Sir!" the Night-Watchman said. "Oi can't think 'ow they gets into t'house."

Clint Wickham was not listening.

He said to the footman:

"Fetch Burton and several more footmen as quickly as you can and tell them to bring ropes with them."

"Very good, Sir!"

The footman was already on his way up the passage as he replied.

"Help me! I need a Physician!" the wounded man spluttered. "I'm in pain! Help me!"

Clint Wickham did not answer.

He merely walked towards the fireplace to stand with his back to it.

"Robbers like these deserves all they gets!" the Night-Watchman was saying. "But wot Oi wants ter know, Sir, is 'ow did they get into t'house? 'T mustn't 'appen again!"

"I shall see that it does not!" Clint Wickham answered.

It was some minutes before the footmen, aroused from their sleep, came hurrying into the Study.

Burton followed, looking strangely unlike his pontifical self in a woollen dressing-gown.

The footmen, on Clint Wickham's instructions, tied up the man who was now recovering consciousness.

The American with the injured wrist, which was bleeding profusely, was being carried away by the footmen.

He was still shouting for a Physician and saying he was in pain.

"Lock them up until morning," Clint Wickham said, "then we will send for the Police and charge them with attempted burglary."

"Very good, Sir, an' 't was extremely fortunate you discovered them before they could do any harm," Burton said.

"I agree," Clint Wickham remarked.

He looked across the room to where the other long knife was still lying on the floor.

"We will need these knives as evidence," he said to Burton, "and I am sure Mr. Trent will see to everything in the morning. It would be a mistake for my guests to know that criminals like these are at large. It might frighten them."

"Yes, of course, Sir, I'll tell the footmen not to

speak of it, and, as you say, Sir, Mr. Trent 'll have them taken away by the Police."

"Thank you, Burton," Clint Wickham said. "I know I can rely on you."

"Of course, Sir," the Butler replied.

He walked to the door, then hesitated.

"Is there anything you need, Sir? A glass of champagne . . . ?"

"No, nothing, thank you," Clint Wickham replied, "I shall be going up to bed in a few moments."

The Butler bowed, and Clint Wickham added:

"I feel that now that these criminals are securely locked up, we can all sleep peacefully."

"Yes, indeed, Sir," Burton replied.

He went from the Study, shutting the door quietly behind him.

Clint Wickham waited until he was quite certain the Butler was on the way to the back premises.

Then with a smile on his lips he went towards the window.

He pulled the curtains apart to see Tila standing where she had been all the time, on the window-seat.

He looked up at her, her fair hair falling over her shoulders.

She was a little pale and her eyes were still frightened at all that had happened.

However, she smiled as they looked at each other.

Clint Wickham put up his arms and lifted her to the ground.

He did not release her, but held her close against him.

She was looking up at him, wanting to say how glad she was that he was safe.

At the same time, words seemed unnecessary.

She had saved him, and that was all that mattered.

For a long moment he looked at her.

Then his arms tightened.

Before she could move, before she could attempt to thrust him away, he was kissing her.

He kissed her wildly, passionately, demandingly, in a manner she had never expected, had never imagined could happen.

He kissed her until she felt as if the room were spinning dizzily around them.

It was impossible to think but only to feel.

In some way she did not understand she was responding to his lips and to the fire that burned in them.

Vaguely she knew that he was conquering her with his kisses.

He was taking what she had refused and making her, whether she agreed or not, part of himself.

When they were both breathless he raised his head.

It was impossible for her to move, impossible to speak.

He looked at her, his eyes blazing.

Then he was kissing her again, kissing her, but more gently than he had done before.

At the same time, she felt as if he drew her heart and soul from her body and made them his.

He had also taken her will from her, and she no longer could think.

She knew only that his kisses gave her the wonder and glory that she had felt when she had looked at the fountain in the sunset.

There were also the stars and the moon which had somehow crept into her breasts.

The glitter of them seemed to sparkle like flames.

He kissed her and went on kissing her.

She felt that if she died, she would have known a feeling that was not human but, in its very ecstasy, Divine.

This was love, the love that was over-whelming, and irresistible.

She was his completely, and she loved him.

It was a love that was different from anything she had imagined, from anything she had read about, or which had been in her dreams.

All she knew was that she was no longer herself, but completely and irrevocably his.

chapter seven

MUCH later Clint said:

"I think you should go to bed, my darling."

They had not spoken for a long time.

Yet Tila felt they had said a million things to each other and there was no need for words.

She stirred against his shoulder and he kissed her forehead, her eyes, her nose, and then the softness of her neck.

He felt the little tremor that ran through her and kissed her lips.

"I love you!" he said. "I love you, so go to bed and dream of me."

He drew her to her feet.

She stood, looking up at him, finding it difficult to understand anything that was said and to come back from Paradise to which he had taken her.

As if he understood, he put his arm round her shoulders and drew her towards the door.

"I have a feeling," he said, "that you know a way

back where you will not be seen. Can you manage alone?"

She nodded.

Once again he kissed her forehead.

Then, as if he forced himself to release her, he stood back, watching her as she moved away down the passage.

She grew fainter and fainter until she disappeared into the darkness at the end of it.

Without really thinking, she went up the narrow staircase by which she had descended.

She walked along a top floor which led her to the School-Room.

Only when she reached her bed-room did she feel as if she was stepping back into reality.

The curtains were drawn back as she had left them.

She went to the window to look at the fountain.

The stars were already beginning to fade in the sky.

She knew in a short while the first fingers of the dawn would appear behind the trees.

It all seemed to be part of her love, the love which pulsated through her whole body.

It was then suddenly, almost as if she had been struck by lightning, that she knew she could no longer stay at Staverly.

If she saw Clint again, she would be helpless and would do everything he asked of her.

He had said he loved her not once, but a hundred times.

His kisses had told her how strong and demanding that love was.

But, at this very moment, lying asleep in one of the State Rooms, was the Duchess's daughter, she who would give him the Dynasty for which he craved.

"I must go . . . away."

Tila did not say the words, but she felt that her Mother said them for her.

She loved Clint.

But how could she do anything which would distress both her Father and Mother and make them ashamed of her?

She turned away from the window, feeling as if the beauty outside was hypnotising her.

She dressed herself quickly, taking down from the wardrobe the first gown she found.

She pinned up her hair at the back of her head, then tip-toed across the landing to enter the School-Room.

She sat down at the table on which there were the books she had taken from the Library.

There was a writing-pad on which she had been inscribing their titles.

Then she wrote hastily but distinctly in her flowing hand-writing:

Dear Emily,

I have to go home because of urgent family affairs. Please take great care of Miss Mary-Lee. I will send later for my luggage. Thank you for being so helpful.

Tila Stevens

She folded the piece of paper over and wrote the name EMILY on it in capitals so that it would not be over-looked.

Then she went back into her bed-room.

She picked up her hand-bag which contained all the money she had brought with her to Staverly.

The rest she had put into the safe at the Dower House.

She went down the stairs from the School-Room Floor, and down another flight.

This brought her near a garden door.

She knew she would not be seen leaving.

A winding path took her through a clump of rhododendron bushes.

She kept out of sight of the windows, just in case anyone should be watching.

She reached the Park, walking in the shadows of the oak trees.

The Dower House was at its edge and outside the village, surrounded by a large garden.

Tila knew the Coblins would be asleep at this hour.

She let herself in through one of the windows which she knew needed mending.

There had been no money to pay for it.

Once she was inside the house, she asked herself if she was doing the right thing.

Even as the question came to her mind, she felt her whole being surge like a tidal wave towards Clint.

"I love . . . you! I love . . . you!" she cried in her heart. "But I cannot . . . spoil our love by . . . doing anything . . . which is wrong."

She found her way to the stairs and climbed up to the landing.

She went into her bed-room, and it was just as she had left it.

The bed had been made, but nothing had been tidied away.

When she pulled back the curtains to let in the light, she could see some of her old clothes still lying on a chair.

The old shoes she wore when she was in the garden were on the floor.

She told herself it did not matter . . . nothing mattered.

Hardly aware of what she was doing, she undressed and, putting on a nightgown, got into bed.

It was then the tears came, and she cried into her pillow until she was exhausted.

"I love him . . . I love . . . him . . . !" she sobbed.

She was still repeating the same words when she fell asleep.

* * *

Tila awoke and thought she heard Mary-Lee calling her.

Then she remembered where she was and that she had run away.

She lay for a long time, aware that it was late in the morning.

The sun was steeping through the sides of the curtains.

There was no hurry, no one knew she was there, and no one would find her.

*   *   *

It was nearly twelve o'clock when Tila went downstairs to the surprise of the Coblins.

"Good 'evans, Miss Otila!" Mrs. Coblin exclaimed. "Where did ye spring from?"

"I came here late last night," Tila explained, "and . . . I am in hiding."

"In 'iding?" Mrs. Coblin repeated. "From who or wot, I'd like to know."

"From everyone!" Tila answered. "I want you both to promise me that you will tell no one I am here. If anyone calls, say you have no idea where I could be."

"Ye're not in trouble, are ye, Miss Otila?" Coblin asked slowly.

"I do not know," Tila answered. "I only want you to hide me . . . and now I think of it . . . I am hungry!"

Mrs. Coblin's mind was instantly diverted.

"I'll get you somethin' t'eat right away, Miss Otila," she said, "an' you're looking a bit 'peaky' now I comes to think of it! Give me quite a shock, you did, turning up like that."

Tila left her busy at the stove and went into the Sitting-Room.

It looked dismal without flowers.

She wondered if it would be safe to go out into the garden and pick some.

Then she asked herself—safe? From whom?

Roby would guess this was where she had gone if he was told she was missing, and Patrick would be angry.

But neither of them would betray her.

Automatically, because it had always been her job, she dusted the Sitting-Room.

She was actually waiting for Mr. Coblin to tell her that her meal was ready.

She did not have to wait long.

Mrs. Coblin had cooked her an omelette because it was quicker than anything else.

There was a salad which had come from the garden.

Tila knew this had been procured by Coblin.

Because he was having good food, he was looking younger and fitter than he had for a long time.

Tila ate the omelette and also the bread-and-butter pudding which followed it.

She smiled as she remembered how she had hated bread-and-butter pudding when she was a child.

But now, as Mrs. Coblin was a good cook, she enjoyed it.

"Thank you," she said to Coblin when she finished.

"It be nice t'have ye back, Miss Otila," he said, "it be lonely wi'out you."

Tila smiled and went out through a door at the back of the house into the garden.

She picked an armful of white lilac and lilies which were just coming into bed.

And there were a few tulips which came up

every year despite the weeds.

She went back into the house.

The front-door was open, and she saw there was a horse tethered to the post outside which her father had put there.

For a moment she stood still.

Then she knew it would be Roby!

Roby would tell her what had happened when Clint Wickham learnt she was missing.

Still holding her flowers, she flung open the Sitting-Room door.

"Roby!" she exclaimed. "Were you worr—"

She stopped.

It was not Roby who was standing at the end of the room, but Clint Wickham.

For a moment her heart seemed to have stopped beating.

Then, because he was there, she felt an irrepressible joy surge up within her.

He did not speak or move. He only stood looking at her.

Because she felt shy, she put her flowers down on the seat of a chair, taking longer over it than was necessary.

As if she knew she had to fight a battle, she took a deep breath and squared her shoulders.

Then she lifted her chin defiantly.

"H-how . . . did you . . . find me?" she asked.

"When I heard you had left," he said, "I could not believe it!"

She walked slowly towards him, and now she stood in front of him.

"I . . . I had to . . . go."

"I thought, after last night, you would understand that I could not live without you."

There was just a pause before Tila said so softly that he could hardly hear:

"Last night was . . . wonderful . . . the most . . . wonderful thing that has . . . ever happened to me . . . but I knew . . . because of it I had to . . . go away."

"Why?"

It was the monosyllable he was so fond of using.

"Because," Tila said, choosing her words carefully, "if I had stayed . . . it would have been . . . impossible not to . . . do what you . . . w-wanted."

"I thought I made what I wanted very clear," Clint answered. "I want you!"

His voice was very deep.

Because she was afraid he might touch her, she moved away from him.

She walked to the window to stare with sightless eyes into the garden.

The sunshine turned her hair to gold, and to Clint watching her, it seemed to give her a halo.

After a long silence, when he did not speak, she said:

"Because I . . . love you . . . and because you . . . make me forget everything in which I . . . believe . . . I had to . . . come away . . . please go . . . go . . . now! We cannot go on . . . arguing and . . . f-fighting."

"That is something I have no intention of doing," Clint answered, "but I suppose I must put into words what I thought I said last night when I kissed you."

Tila held her breath.

"It is quite simply," he said quietly, "how soon, my darling, will you marry me?"

Tila felt she could not have heard aright.

Could it be possible that Clint Wickham, after all he had said about his "Dynasty" with a Duchess's daughter waiting for him, had actually asked her to *marry* him?

It flashed through her mind that it was the most wonderful thing that could happen.

He was prepared to marry, not Otila Staverly, who at least had some standing in the Social World, but "Miss Stevens," an impoverished Governess who had nothing to recommend her except her imagination.

Even as she felt her heart leap because he loved her so much, she thought perhaps it was a mistake.

Later he might regret it.

"Have . . . you . . . forgotten," she said in a voice that trembled, "your . . . Dynasty?"

She did not turn round so did not see him smile.

"Yes, I have thought about that," he answered, "and I intend to have my Dynasty!"

Tila felt herself freeze.

So she *had* been mistaken in what he said. Then she started.

Without being aware of it, he had crossed the room and was standing just behind her.

"I *shall* have my Dynasty," he replied, "only a little different from how I planned it previously. But I think you will appreciate it as much as I will."

It was impossible for Tila to move or speak.

He put out his hands and turned her round to face him.

She thought when she looked at him he seemed different.

Then she realised that it was because she had never seen him look so happy.

"We will start a Dynasty, my lovely one," he said, "and it will be a Dynasty of Love."

Then, before she could answer, he pulled her into his arms and his lips found hers.

He kissed her until once again she was flying in the sky.

Only this was even more wonderful, more perfect than it had been before.

When he raised his head she managed to ask a little incoherently:

"Do . . . you . . . doyou . . . reallymean . . . that?"

"I mean it!" he said. "And our Dynasty, yours and mine, my precious, will be a link which will cross the Atlantic and will unite not only ourselves but our countries with love."

He would have kissed her again, but she put her hands on his chest to hold him off.

"Are . . . you certain . . . quite . . . certain," she asked, "that you will not . . . regret when it is . . . too late that I am not . . . a Duke's daughter?"

"I shall regret nothing!" Clint said firmly. "But if you ever run away from me again I shall go mad!"

"H-how . . . did you find . . . me?" Tila asked after a moment. "Did . . . Roby tell you . . . where I might . . . be?"

"Staverly? Did you tell *him* you were coming here?"

There was a note in his voice as if he was suddenly suspicious.

Tila realised incredulously that he still had no idea that Roby was her brother.

She was about to speak when Clint went on:

"I learnt from Mary-Lee that you had disappeared. She come to me in tears to say that you had gone, and fortunately I was alone in the Study."

"I did not . . . want her . . . to be . . . upset," Tila murmured.

"Of course she was upset. 'I love Miss Stevens, Poppa,' she said to me. 'You must get her back! I would hate any other Governess!' "

"So that . . . is how . . . you knew," Tila said. "What . . . did you . . . do then?"

Clint smiled.

"I used my imagination."

"How?"

"It was not so very difficult. If you left the house last night after you had left me, it was unlikely that you would have ordered a carriage or ridden a horse."

He paused and went on:

"I decided you must have walked, and that meant you lived on the Estate or else in the village."

"It was . . . stupid of me not to . . . realise that was . . . what you would . . . think."

"I somehow had the feeling you were thinking of me, and because I wanted you so desperately, you drew me by what the Indians called the 'Power of

Thought' to where you were hiding."

Tila gave a little cry.

"That is a lovely idea! So that is . . . why you came . . . here!"

"I told no one where I was going," Clint said. "I went to the stables and just rode straight here."

"Then you have not had any luncheon!" Tila exclaimed. "And what will all your guests think?"

"Quite frankly, I am not interested," Clint said. "I have found you, and if you had not been here, I would have gone on looking for you without giving them another thought!"

Tila laughed.

"Poor Patrick! He has taken so much trouble in trying to make you socially important."

"He has done quite well for himself," Clint replied, "and if I no longer require his services, he will doubtless find somebody else."

Tila looked at him enquiringly, and he added:

"Yes, I am well aware he has made a great deal of money out of 'sponsoring' me, if that is the right word."

It was then with a feeling of horror that Tila remembered what her own part had been in the arrangement.

Moving like a child who is suddenly frightened, she hid her face against him.

"I have . . . something to . . . tell you," she murmured.

His arms tightened around her.

"If it was the reason you were downstairs last night," he said, "I have guessed it already."

"H-how could . . . you . . . guess?"

"When I knew that Patrick was in communication with my worst enemy, I suspected he would put a spy somewhere in the vicinity."

He kissed the top of Tila's head before he said:

"But I had not the slightest idea that she would look or be like you, my darling!"

"You are not . . . shocked and you have . . . not stopped . . . loving me?" Tila asked.

"That is a very good question," Clint answered, "but you know as well as I do that it would be impossible for either of us to stop loving each other."

He put his fingers under her chin to turn her face up to his.

"You even loved me when you walked away from me to come here!"

"I came *because* . . . I love you," Tila whispered. "How could we . . . spoil anything so . . . perfect as our love which . . . comes from God?"

"I knew that was what you were thinking," Clint said, "and although it seems incredible, that is what I think too!"

"Oh, Clint . . . is that really . . . true?"

"You would know if I were lying," he answered, "and that is something we must never do to each other again, and there will be no secrets between us."

"I . . . hated the . . . idea in the . . . first place," Tila said.

"But think, if you had not gone to the Study last night," Clint reminded her, "you would not have been able to save me, and I am very thankful, my precious love, that those two men who I know now

158

are responsible for a great many crimes in America will never trouble us again."

"What about . . . the man who . . . sent them?" Tila asked in a frightened voice.

"If I am in danger in the future, I am sure you will save me, but I promise I shall take every precaution, wherever we may be."

Before she could speak, he pulled her closer against him and said:

"I know you want to explore the world, and that is something we are going to do, besides a great many other things."

Tila gave a little murmur of happiness, and he went on:

"The sooner we can be married the better. It seems incredible, but I have never asked you if you have any family."

"It seems even more incredible," Tila answered, "that you do not know that Roby is my brother!"

For a moment Clint just stared at her.

"Are you telling me that you are a Staverly?" he asked.

Tila smiled.

"Otila Staverly," she said softly.

"I suppose I might have guessed it," Clint exclaimed. "It never seemed right that a Governess called 'Stevens' could look like you, or be so brilliantly intelligent so that I have lain awake trying to polish up my brain!"

"I do not believe a word of it!" Tila said. "But, darling, wonderful Clint, if I have to compete with a Duke's daughter who no longer interests you, I have to have a few weapons of defence."

"Otila Staverly!" Clint said. "I like that—I like that very much!"

"You are thinking of your Dynasty!" Tila teased.

"I think of that when I am kissing you, and when we are married you will realise it is more important than anything else."

As he spoke, there was a touch of fire in his eyes.

Because she understood what he meant, she blushed and hid her face against him.

"I am still waiting for an answer to my question," he said.

"We shall have to ask Roby. Both Papa and Mama are dead and Roby is therefore my Guardian. I am afraid he is going to find it hard to believe that the 'Almighty Wickham' who has done so much for Staverly intends to become a permanent part of his family!"

"A very permanent part," Clint averred, "and I am already thinking how well it will all work out."

Tila looked up at him enquiringly, and he explained:

"Roby can look after the Estate for me, and live in this nice little house. He can move into Staverly when we are away, which will be frequently, and, as I know that the one thing he longs to do is to ride my horses, it all fits into place like a jig-saw puzzle."

"Of course it does!" Tila cried. "And it is wonderful of you to think of everything that will make not only me happy, but also Roby."

"I know another little person who will be happy," Clint said as he smiled, "and that is Mary-Lee."

Tila looked up at him anxiously.

"You are quite certain she will not mind me taking her . . . mother's place in . . . your life?"

"Mary-Lee was so worried when you disappeared that I know she loves you," Clint replied, "and she is, I assure you, happier with you than anybody else who has looked after her."

He drew Tila a little closer as he said:

"I think Mary-Lee should have brothers and sisters to play with, and there is plenty of room for them all at Staverly as well as in my houses in America."

Tila blushed and looked shy, and he thought no one could look more beautiful.

"My precious, my darling!" he said. "How can I have been such a fool as to think I could be happy with anyone but you!"

Tila put her hand up to touch his cheek, and he said:

"I have not had time to tell you, but I made a great mistake in my first marriage, and if my wife had not died, we would undoubtedly have had a divorce."

He took Tila's hand in his and kissed her fingers before he went on:

"I decided then that if I married again, it would be for advantageous reasons—a Marriage of Convenience—like the French and, of course, a lot of English Aristocrats."

"Roby told me," Tila said, "that there are a number of them going to America to look for rich American wives."

"That is what gave me the idea of reversing the

process," Clint said, "and coming to England to find an aristocratic bride."

"And that is what Patrick thought was a good idea." Tila smiled.

"He worked it all out for me," Clint said, "but of course, he forgot, as I did, that I might unexpectedly, and for me incredibly, fall wildly, passionately, in love with the most beautiful person I have ever seen!"

"Oh, Clint . . . are you . . . sure you . . . love me enough?"

"Enough for what?" he asked. "To be sure that I shall be happy for the rest of my life? To know that nothing else is important except that you love me?"

"That is what . . . I want," Tila murmured.

"Then what are we waiting for?"

He got to his feet, pulling Tila to hers at the same time.

"What are . . . you saying? What are you . . . doing?" she asked.

"We are going to find your Brother and tell him we are going to be married immediately, in fact as soon as Mr. Trent, who will leave as soon as we reach the house, can return with a Special Licence!"

"Can we . . . really do . . . that?"

"It is what we *will* do!" he said with the note of determination in his voice she knew so well.

She was looking up at him, and her eyes seemed to hold the sunshine.

"I suppose you know," she said, "that I have . . . no clothes for a trousseau, and obviously no time to buy any?"

Clint laughed.

"We will buy them together in Paris, and I shall enjoy making you look even lovelier whether you are clothed in sunshine or enveloped with stars."

As if he could not help himself, he pulled her into his arms.

He kissed her in the same fierce, wild, passionate way he had kissed her last night.

She felt as she had then that her whole being responded to him and she became part of him.

"I love . . . you! I love . . . you!"

The words vibrated in her heart, and she knew his heart was saying the same thing.

They were flying into the sky, blinded by the sun, and moving as he had thought last night towards the Gates of Heaven.

She knew that when they married they would pass through them.

Then nothing would matter because they were One.

ABOUT THE AUTHOR

Barbara Cartland, the world's most famous romantic novelist, who is also an historian, playwright, lecturer, political speaker and television personality, has now written over 547 books and sold over six hundred and twenty million copies all over the world.

She has also had many historical works published and has written four autobiographies as well as the biographies of her mother and that of her brother, Ronald Cartland, who was the first Member of Parliament to be killed in the last war. This book has a preface by Sir Winston Churchill and has just been republished with an introduction by Sir Arthur Bryant.

Love at the Helm, a novel written with the help and inspiration of the late Earl Mountbatten of Burma, Great Uncle of His Royal Highness The Prince of Wales, is being sold for the Mountbatten Memorial Trust.

She has broken the world record for the last sixteen

years by writing an average of twenty-three books a year. In the *Guinness Book of Records* she is listed as the world's top-selling author.

Miss Cartland in 1978 sang an Album of Love Songs with the Royal Philharmonic Orchestra.

In private life Barbara Cartland, who is a Dame of the Order of St. John of Jerusalem, Chairman of the St. John Council in Hertfordshire and Deputy President of the St. John Ambulance Brigade, has fought for better conditions and salaries for Midwives and Nurses.

She championed the cause for the Elderly in 1956 invoking a Government Enquiry into the "Housing Condition of Old People."

In 1962 she had the Law of England changed so that Local Authorities had to provide camps for their own Gypsies. This has meant that since then thousands and thousands of Gypsy children have been able to go to School, which they had never been able to do in the past, as their caravans were moved every twenty-four hours by the Police.

There are now fourteen camps in Hertfordshire and Barbara Cartland has her own Romany Gypsy Camp called Barbaraville by the Gypsies.

Her designs "Decorating with Love" are being sold all over the U.S.A. and the National Home Fashions League made her, in 1981, "Woman of Achievement."

She is unique in that she was one and two in the Dalton list of Best Sellers, and one week had four books in the top twenty.

Barbara Cartland's book *Getting Older, Growing*

Younger has been published in Great Britain and the U.S.A. and her fifth cookery book, *The Romance of Food*, is now being used by the House of Commons.

In 1984 she received at Kennedy Airport America's Bishop Wright Air Industry Award for her contribution to the development of aviation. In 1931 she and two R.A.F. Officers thought of, and carried, the first aeroplane-towed glider airmail.

During the War she was Chief Lady Welfare Officer in Bedfordshire, looking after 20,000 Service men and women. She thought of having a pool of Wedding Dresses at the War Office so a Service Bride could hire a gown for the day.

She bought 1,000 gowns without coupons for the A.T.S., the W.A.A.F.'s and the W.R.E.N.S. In 1945 Barbara Cartland received the Certificate of Merit from Eastern Command.

In 1964 Barbara Cartland founded the National Association for Health of which she is the President, as a front for all the Health Stores and for any product made as alternative medicine.

This is now a £65 million turnover a year, with one-third going in export.

In January 1988 she received *La Médaille de Vermeil de la Ville de Paris*. This is the highest award to be given in France by the City of Paris. She has sold 25 million books in France.

In March 1988 Barbara Cartland was asked by the Indian Government to open their Health Resort outside Delhi. This is almost the largest Health Resort in the world.

Barbara Cartland was received with great enthusiasm by her fans, who feted her at a reception in the City, and she received the gift of an embossed plate from the Government.

Barbara Cartland was made a Dame of the Order of the British Empire in the 1991 New Year's Honours List by Her Majesty, The Queen, for her contribution to Literature and also for her years of work for the community.